LEAVE JANELLE

SARAH SPADE

Cover by Jessica Lynch

FOREWORD

Thank you for checking out *Leave Janelle*, the prequel to the *Claws and Fangs* series!

In the first full-length book, *Never His Mate*, Gemma mentions her mother as an example that fated mates don't always work out. Though her fated mate was Jack "Wicked Wolf" Walker, the Alpha of the Western Pack, Janelle left him when Gem was a young pup. She eventually chose to bond with Paul Booker, the Alpha of the Lakeview Pack, and the shifter who adopted Gem.

This novella is set about twenty-five years before Gem and Ryker's romance. It tells the story of Janelle escaping her abusive mate, as well as how she met—and fell in love with—Paul. It's a rejected mates story where the fated mates don't end up together, because sometimes fate gets it wrong and it's much better to follow your heart instead.

I do have a few content warnings for this novella (also noted in the description on the sales page). This story includes: domestic violence, implied sexual assault (spousal rape), and mentions of murder (it occurs off page, but Jack really is one hell of a socio-pathic prick). Janelle does get her HEA with Paul, but she goes through a lot to get there and I want to make sure anyone reading this story knows what to expect beforehand.

Thanks again, and enjoy!

xoxo,

Sarah

1

The front door to my cabin slams closed and, going right where it hurts the most, I gingerly lift the hem of my ripped and bloody blouse.

I know better than to look while Jack is still in the cabin with me. It'll only ramp up his desire if I react to the marks he leaves behind, and after three years of being forced to mate whenever he's in the mood, I do what is expected of me.

No more.

No less.

I know what gets him off, and I know that even the smallest whimper is enough to ensure that he'll pound harder, bite deeper, and he won't leave my bed until he's come at least twice.

He likes it when I whimper.

When I scream. When I cry.

My pain turns him on, and the mating becomes as fierce and as wild and as cruel as he is. Whoever first gave him his name of Wicked Wolf Walker was probably an enemy rather than a bedmate, but they got it right anyway. Even when he's in his skin, he's more beastly than any other wolf I've ever known.

For three years, he's pushed me to take his marks. There isn't an inch on my body that hasn't been scored up by his claws at some point, but I refuse to accept a single scar. I might be his fated mate. I might be the female he claims as his, even when he's stalking out of my cabin to visit a much more willing packmate. But until I wear his marks and let him fuck me under the Luna's watchful gaze, I'm not irrevocably tied to him for the rest of my life.

Jack is a contradiction. His possessive streak demands that I give in to him, accepting his mark and becoming his bonded mate with the whole pack as witness. But he's insatiable, too, and he knows that if we *do* perform the Luna Ceremony, I won't only be stuck with him.

He'll be stuck with me.

And since the idea of being tied to one female for life is probably the only thing in this world that... I won't say *frightens* because he's not afraid of anything... that *concerns* him, Jack fucks me and he marks me and he knows as well as I do that, when he's in the mood, he'll get to do it all over again. And he'll do it with the tips of his canine fangs burrowing into his bottom lip as his gold shifter's eyes turn molten with lust and excitement.

But that's later. I know he'll return much sooner than I'd like. He always does. Until then, I need to check the damage from his last rutting.

Taking a deep breath, I inch the ruined shirt higher. That breath turns into a wince when I see the mess he's made of my belly and my side. Four jagged tears split my skin, wrapping around to my back. Remembering the way he gripped me as he pounded into me, I'm sure the claw on his thumb has burrowed nearly into my freaking kidney.

It certainly feels like it.

Another breath. I can already see the wound knitting together around the edges. Give it an hour and there'll be no sign that the marks were ever there.

A shaky exhale as I realize that it could've been worse.

It *has* been worse.

Jack was actually in a pretty decent mood today. He was gentle as he mounted me, and though I've learned to expect the cuts, the gouges, the marks, he barely nibbled on my shoulder as he pinned me beneath his powerful body. He marked me because of course he did—he'll never *not* take the opportunity to do so—but it was almost like an afterthought.

It could've been worse—

My senses ping. As I sit on the edge of my bed, my inner wolf cocks her head, suddenly alert. I could've sworn I heard something in the main room of my cabin just then and, before I can figure out what it could be, a small blonde pup pokes her snout in past the open door to my bedroom.

I should've known better. Only a year old and my daughter is a pro at tracking and stalking. Unlike some other pups, she is almost noiseless in her approach, plus she smells so much like me that I often find it difficult to scent her in the cabin—a fact which her wolf instinctively seems to understand. I'm her favorite target, and normally I adore that.

Normally—but not when I'm recovering from another one of her father's visits.

She shouldn't be here. As soon as I could sense Jack coming to the cabin, I put her down for a nap. He was quick today, as if he had other places to be and was just stopping in for an afternoon mating, so she should still be in her crib. I don't even pause to wonder how she got out, though. Seeing her in her shifted form tells me all I need to know.

A keening whine escapes her. When she's in her skin, she can say a few words: Mama. Wolf. Play. In her fur? She's even more expressive. That one high-pitched

4

cry tells me that she knows I'm hurt, and that she wants to do something to help me.

She *knows*, but she doesn't have to see. I quickly lower my shirt, careful to cover up the healing marks. Then, before she can think I'm ignoring her, I whistle softly through my teeth.

Ruby bounds into my room. Her ears are flat against her skull, her tiny canine fangs bared as if she expected to find an enemy in here with me.

She isn't wrong.

My heart breaks for her. I hide that, too, pasting an encouraging smile on my face as I pat my lap. "Ah, baby. Come here, Ruby girl."

She runs for me, rearing back and leaping to make the jump before curling up in my lap. I feel her snuffling breath as her nose pokes through the rips in my blouse, then the soft tentative lick of her warm tongue when she finds the marks. Then, when she scents her father on my skin, she rumbles with a growl.

My girl. My poor, poor pup.

I run my trembling fingers through her soft, downy fur. "Why aren't you sleeping, Ruby? It's nap time."

Tapping into my inner wolf, I can use the bond between mother and pup to... encourage her to sleep through the worst of what happens when Jack comes to our cabin. Her true nature is making it harder and harder, though. Too young to know why I'm so desperate to protect her, my daughter's instincts are already revving her to protect me instead.

But that's not her job. And, if I have it my way, it never will be.

She lifts up her head, a tiny alpha wolf who—despite being barely one—is more dominant than I'll ever be.

Though I know it'll slow the healing of my marks, I pour more of my omega aura over Ruby. From the moment I recognized directly after her birth that she was different, that she was *special*, I've done everything possible to hide the truth of her nature.

As far back as pack lore goes, there's only ever been one born female alpha wolf: the Luna, our goddess that ascended millennia ago and who is worshipped as the moon in the sky. She was stronger than any other alpha, she could control any wolf with only her howl, and she had the ability to choose a mate and make him a god in his own right. Simply put: she's the greatest of our kind and revered as such.

And maybe the story of the Luna is just that. A story. A legend. A myth. It could be, but if there's one thing I'm sure of, it's this: my pup is as much an alpha as her father, and if any other shifter discovered the truth, she wouldn't be my pup any longer. Whether Jack put her down as a threat or our people thought of her as the second coming of the Luna, I don't know, but I'm not willing to risk it.

I'm not willing to risk *her*.

I pick my daughter up, nuzzling her with my cheek. As I do, she shifts back to her skin. I adjust my hold on her as Ruby glances up at me. Her honey gold eyes are a little bit glassy; she must've woken up from her sleep and run right to me. Her pudgy fingers reach for my long, brown hair. My scalp is sensitive from where Jack yanked as he mated me, but if Ruby wants to pull my hair to get closer to me, that's fine. She might be an alpha wolf, but she's also a confused child who needs to be reassured by her mama.

This is all my fault. When I became pregnant—a shock since we're mates, but we're not *bonded* mates—I thought this might be my chance. That Jack might finally change. Be the mate I always dreamed of, and the father my pup deserved.

But as proud as he was to have knocked me up in the first place, that all changed when I had Ruby. He was furious that I dare give him a daughter instead of a son to carry on his legacy, and when I boldly lied and said she was an omega, I thought he might kill us both.

To my surprise, he didn't. And then I thought that maybe he might finally forsake us, that I might finally be free from him, but he didn't reject us, either.

Sometimes, I wish he had. Because while I've successfully hidden the truth about my daughter from him this last year, I'm not so sure I'll be able to much longer.

And if he discovers that his pup is an alpha like him... something that is supposed to be *impossible*—

No. I don't even want to think about it.

Instead, I squeeze my Ruby to my chest, burrowing my nose in her blonde curls.

Jack can force me. Hit me. Carve me up like so much meat. He can put me down for not being the female he believes *he* deserves. He can flaunt our broken mating by fucking every available female pack-mate in his free time like he has a habit of doing. Whether he's trying to prove something to me or the rest of the pack, I don't know. I don't care, either. So long as my girl's safe, I'll deal with it.

I'll deal with it all.

Spinning in circles, Ruby snaps her baby fangs at the tip of her blonde tail. She's not fast enough to catch it, and she ends up with a few pieces of fur sticking out of her muzzle as she chuffs happily.

It's been a couple of hours since Jack left. Bringing Ruby into the bathroom with me, I took a quick shower to rinse off as much of his scent as I could. I made sure to open the windows before I did to help air out the bedroom. She seemed to settle down once the reminder of her father was gone. My marks were almost completely faded, too, and as soon as I threw out the ripped and bloody blouse, Ruby shifted back to her fur.

Her good mood is contagious. Feeling a bit better myself, I fed her—and once she was content, I made myself some lunch, too—and tried to put her down for another nap, but she refused to leave my side. Instead, she's amusing the both of us as she chases her tail.

My pup spends most of her time as a wolf. I don't blame her. As a human, she can walk now, but that's about all. Her reflexes are far more keen when she's shifted, and her senses have only grown over the last few months.

Most pups don't have their first shift until they've reached at least a year. Ruby was a wolf by the time she was four months old, and while that's not unheard of, it's usually a mark of an alpha.

The fact that no one's ever heard of a female alpha —save for the Luna—works in my favor. It's impossible, therefore no one ever guesses that Ruby is anything other than what I present her as: an advanced omega. Besides, I'm the only omega that currently lives in the Western Pack. Most of my packmates know diddly squat when it comes to my kind of wolf so it doesn't take much to explain away some of Ruby's idiosyncrasies.

Of course, that was when she was much younger. Lately, she gets more and more questioning looks on the rare occasions I let her out of the cabin, and though the pack gossips stay far away from me and my pup thanks to her father, I can sense their growing curiosity.

That's why I prefer to stay inside the cabin with Ruby. Openly disappointed with an omega mate and an omega pup, Jack encourages us to keep out of sight. He sends some of the less dominant packmates—those who worship the ground the Alpha walks on and who would never question his commands—to make sure we have everything we need; Luna forbid any of the pack think he doesn't provide for his mate. But just because I'd rather keep out of sight, sometimes there's no avoiding it.

Later that afternoon, I realize that I'm out of milk. And I know I should wait until one of Jack's runners stops by, but Ruby gave up on chasing her tail a while ago. When she shifted back to her skin, using two of the words she's most fondest of—"Walk, Mama, walk" —I decide that going to the District store for milk is as good an excuse as any to let her get some fresh air.

Everything is going fine until we leave the more secluded part of pack territory where my cabin is and enter the crowded center of the square. Ruby doesn't shift, though she does stop short, nearly tripping over her unsteady feet as something catches her attention.

A second later, I pick up on the same familiar scent that she must have.

Jack.

I search the crowd ahead of us, but I don't see him —and, believe me, there's no missing that male. However, when I follow my nose, I see a pretty redhead glaring at me from about twenty feet away.

Ah, Sandy McGee. I should've known.

Sandy is one of Jack's girls. Even from this distance, I can smell him all over her.

Well... at least now I know where he ran off to after he left me bloody and marked earlier.

As soon as she sees that she has my attention, Sandy sniffs noticeably, then snaps her blunt human teeth at me.

Yup. Despite my shower, she can smell him on me, too.

Sandy is considered a delta wolf. A basic pack member. Compared to Jack and his ever-changing retinue of Betas, her dominance level is much closer to mine. She doesn't have the gentle nature that belongs to my rank, and she proves it by continuing to glare at me as if she wants nothing more than to fight me for the right to be Jack's mate.

If only she knew that I'd change positions with her in a heartbeat—and not just because of her status.

I'm an omega wolf, but I'm also the Omega here. In some packs, it's a status that is almost as highly ranked as the alpha. Not in the Western Pack. Here, in the hidden community known as the Wolf District, my nature is seen as a weakness all because Jack believes that.

Still, no one in the Wolf District will challenge me. Why bother? I can't get any lower than the bottom, and my status as Jack's sole fated mate means that I have a tiny bit of protection against his jealous bedmates. I'm the mother of his pup, the mate the Luna chose for him, and even if he gets perverse enjoyment out of making me bleed, he'll tear the throat out of anyone who tries to lay a claw on me.

Not out of love, though. It's possession. I'm his, and even if he fucks every available female—and some not so available, except to the Alpha—in the Wolf District, I'm off-limits. Just... not in the way that omega wolves usually are.

Not like he needs to use me as an excuse to come down hard on any packmate he feels is questioning him. Whether it's his leadership as pack Alpha or his relationship with me, Jack reacts swiftly to even the tiniest hint of a challenge against him.

Swiftly, and cruelly.

So, instead of lowering my gaze and giving Sandy the satisfaction that she's bullied the weak Omega, I tuck a strand of hair behind my ear and smile warmly at her.

She can have Jack if she wants him. Nothing would make me happier than for him to decide to break our mating, rejecting me to choose another. I could move back to the midwest with Ruby, leaving the Wolf District far, far behind me.

But that'll never happen. I know it. So does Sandy.

Still, I smile, and when another of Jack's girls glares daggers at my pup and me, I smile at her, too.

I'm an omega. Honestly, it's all I *can* do.

2

I'm not being the least bit dramatic when I say that the cycle of the moon is the bane of my existence.

You'd think that, as a shifter, I would be used to it by now. Though us wolves can change between fur and skin whenever we want to, there's something about the full moon that rules us. Whether it's because we revere the Luna as our goddess, or if her pull controls our inner beasts the same way the moon controls the tide, I'm not sure. It doesn't matter. When the Luna hangs heavy in the sky, we *are* our beasts.

We fight. We fuck. We feast.

And, most importantly, it's on the night of the full moon that I can be trapped with Jack forever.

The Luna Ceremony is simple enough. For a shifter to bond with their mate, there needs to be a marking, then a claiming with the Luna as witness. If she blesses your mating—and she always does, especially when it's fated—then the bond snaps into place and the pair is bonded.

Together.

Forever.

For three years, I've been careful to avoid Jack on the night of the full moon. Though my human side refuses to be tied to him until death do us part, I'm still an omega wolf. He's the Alpha. As much as I hate to admit it, if he pushes it, my inner wolf would show him her throat, then whine until he mounts me. I'd be helpless to stop it—and then we'd be bonded before the full moon set. My senses would return with the daylight, but the damage would be done. Literally, too, since any mark made during the Luna Ceremony would stay as a scar that would never heal even if I willed it to.

Just further proof that he isn't interested in having a bonded mate. Even on the few times that he demanded to rut when the moon was full, he didn't mark me. Oh, no. He always saves his bites and his slashes and his claw marks for every other night of the year because he doesn't want to settle for any one female. Why would he when, as Alpha, he could have countless?

Of course, as both his intended and his fated mate, the Luna has her own way of tying us together. Until he rejects me fully, choosing to bond to another female and finally setting me free, I'm the only one who can bear him a pup. All it took was him mating me during the height of the full moon one time and I fell pregnant.

I hadn't known that was even possible. Pack lore said that only bonded mates could create pups, but Jack boasted that he was such a powerful alpha wolf shifter, even the Luna wanted him to spread his seed and continue to grow his pack before he settled down with me for good.

But then none of his other bedmates could conceive, and when my pup was finally born, he was disgusted to find that she took after me. Our daughter was another omega. A weakling. A disgrace.

And if I've spent the last year doing everything in my ability to keep up that facade, it's worth it.

All the times Jack took his aggression out on me. All the times he ignored Ruby entirely before ordering me to all fours so that I could give him a worthy pup instead of an omega runt. All the times I struggled to heal the marks he left behind because I was using too much of my omega nature to cover up the truth of what type of wolf my Ruby really is... it's all worth it because the alternative is simply unfathomable.

Still, I've learned how to manage my mate during the full moon. Jack's temper and his lusts and the way the Luna affects my wolf aren't why I dread her appearance. Not entirely.

Nope. It's my poor baby.

It takes so much out of me and my wolf to conceal Ruby in the days leading up to the full moon because —as I first discovered when I came to live as Jack's mate—an alpha is even more affected by her than the rest of the pack.

Jack, in particular, is a *monster*.

His wolf has always been more vicious than most. The Western Pack excuses it because an Alpha must be strong, must be protective, must be a fighter, but I've always believed there's a line between an Alpha and a vicious killer. Jack Walker is firmly on the other side of that line.

His mood is pretty volatile on the best of days, but during the full moon? I'm not the only one who goes easy like I'm padding on broken glass. It's not unusual for a packmate or two to go missing, and when the current Beta—because Jack just can't seem to keep a right-hand wolf at his side—inevitably asks what happened to them, his answer is always the same: "We went hunting."

Only there's never any meat, and the missing packmates never return. Considering his obsession with growing the pack so that it's not only the largest pack in the West but in all the States, if I didn't already know that Jack was a sadistic sociopath, that would've been one hell of a clue.

That's not all, either. As the pack Omega, I have an empathic ability unique to my status. Just like how I can attempt to calm certain packmates—or, in the case of Ruby, use my ranking to shield hers—I can also sense how they're feeling. An unstable Alpha leads to some of the more dominant shifters losing control. Riled up in response to Jack's alpha aura, they get the brilliant idea to challenge him.

And, of course, he just has to put them down. With the whole pack serving as witness to his power, Jack often uses the full moon as an excuse to rip those wolves apart as a warning to any would-be alphas that to challenge him was to beg for death.

Even worse, he insists that I be present, front and center, for every challenge fight. As his intended, these brutal bouts are supposed to be his way of proving that he's both the strongest male in the pack and the perfect mate for me.

But if he was? He'd know that being forced to watch another wolf be ripped to shreds has exactly the opposite effect on an omega.

My kind is historically coddled, but for good reason. Omegas can usually soothe any of their more dominant packmates, but even the most bloodthirsty wolf is a pussycat when compared to Wicked Wolf Walker.

I know why he does it. It's punishment. Even if Jack doesn't want to be formally bonded to me any more than I want to be tied to him, he's punishing me for every full moon that I refuse to perform the Luna Ceremony with him. He hunts and he fights and he'll find someone else to rut with regardless, but he makes me pay every single time the Luna appears.

I take that, too. I have no choice. The fights weren't as common before Ruby—when I could use all of my omega nature to soothe Jack so that he only took his aggression out on me and not the whole pack—but since then? As awful as it is, I made a choice. To protect my pup, I knew I had to sacrifice my minor hold on her father. I couldn't calm him, and he's only gotten worse in the moons since she was born.

The last full moon, Jack spent the afternoon into the early evening with Portia, and by the time he decided it was my turn, he was intercepted, then challenged by a young alpha who had recently joined the pack.

The boy was barely eighteen. No match for Jack. Knowing that, the Alpha didn't bother calling the pack together to watch him. He didn't even shift. Relying on just his claws, he beckoned the boy close before gutting him, then ripping out his throat. As he gargled on his blood, Jack stepped over him and, with barely a hitch in his stride, he stalked the rest of the way to my cabin.

With an unholy amount of perverse pleasure, he gleefully told me how it took longer for the boy to die than it did for Jack to kill him. Then, his eyes lighting up when he saw the horror I couldn't hide, he smirked and, using the same bloody claws, sliced my skirt to pieces.

And though he usually prefers to make me go on all fours so that he can fuck me from behind, the sick bastard ordered me to my bed, pushing me to my back. He laid on top of me, shoving himself inside of me as he licked the tears from my cheeks.

It was just another reminder that there isn't a single part of me that doesn't belong to him.

Jack likes it when I cry, especially when it's because of an emotional hurt rather than a physical one. Over the years, I've gotten used to the pain.

I thought I had gotten used to his cruelty, too, but I was wrong.

That's the thing about the Wicked Wolf of the West. Whenever I think that he can't be crueler, he glories in proving me wrong. Honestly, except for when he's flexing his dominance over those weaker than him, it's the only time I ever really sense any true happiness coming from him.

That should have been enough. The pleasure he got from killing a kid—and his enjoyment at how I cried over his inhumanity—should have been enough to make me realize that I couldn't keep playing my games with Jack forever. I might have managed to avoid being forced into bonding myself to him these last three years, but I've been fooling myself if I thought he wouldn't grow tired of it and push me to say yes.

I thought I had a little more time, though.

Turns out, I didn't.

ALL TOO SOON, IT'S ANOTHER MONTH.

Another cycle.

Another full moon.

Even if I didn't know she was coming, I could sense the Luna's approach. It's a shifter thing. My whole body is vibrating, the little hairs on the back of my neck standing straight as I try to shake off my body's needs.

I need to shift. I need to run. I need to let my wolf side take over, and I need to throw my head back and bay up at her.

More than all of that, though, I ache with the desire to let my mate mount me and rut away.

Whenever it's this close to the full moon, it's a struggle not to give in to the demands of my wolf. As much as she knows that our mate is no good for us, she's always been blinded by the large blond wolf with the sharp fangs and the possessive gleam in his bright gold eyes.

Every moon since Jack marched into the territory of my former pack, claiming me in front of everyone I've ever known, then bringing me back with him to the Wolf District, I've fought the urge to let him mark me. It was harder in the early days, and only his initial refusal to bond an omega to him outright kept me safe. Later, I did everything I could to stop him, and though it's so incredibly difficult when the Luna is out, I think of Ruby and I manage.

I *have* to.

I got lucky this month. Leading up to this full moon, he's been busy with pack business. Three days ago, he left for the annual pack meet where every Alpha gets together to posture and threaten and, in some cases, make alliances. Some Alphas bring their families with them, but not Jack. I'm weak, therefore I'm a weakness. And the fewer people who know that his pup appears to be another omega, the better.

Since he left, the whisper-thin bond between us is stretched taut, leading out of the Wolf District. The pack meet ended last night, and though he's not back home yet, he will be soon. I can sense his approach like an oncoming train.

It's rushing, it can roll right over me, and there isn't a Luna damned thing I can do to avoid it.

He'll be back by tomorrow's full moon. I'm sure of it. No pack meet ever lasts through a full moon, and even if I could pretend it might, I got confirmation that he's already on his way back to our territory from the Beta of the Western Pack.

Jack's most recent Beta is a cocky wolf about ten years older than I am. Scott took over when Caleb couldn't hack the position any longer. I try not to focus on the fact that I haven't seen claw nor fang of Caleb since he told Jack he wanted out of the job three months ago.

It's... it's easier that way.

Scott is definitely a good match for Jack. There's a vindictive gleam in his dark eyes that reminds me far too much of the Alpha, and if rumors hold true, he's got a sadistic streak a mile wild.

And that's not the only thing he has in common with the Alpha.

Last night, Scott came by to see me. He told me to expect Jack some time today—just like he told me that, if I was lonely while I waited for my mate to return, he was more than happy to warm my bed until Jack was back.

He wants to fuck me, and he's willing to risk Jack's notorious temper for a chance. I could sense lust oozing off of him even before he made his offer. Determination, too. Like he believed that, if he could convince the Alpha's mate to choose him, he might have a shot at challenging Jack for control of the pack next.

It'll never happen, and not just because I appear to be completely loyal to Jack.

I've only ever been with one male and that's my mate; whether I'd choose him or not doesn't change the fact that, for now, Jack Walker *is* my mate. I was barely twenty when the Luna told him that I was his intended mate and he came to retrieve me. Though he had his choice of tracking down his fated mate or choosing one of his own, he went with fate—even when he discovered that an omega was the female meant for him.

It was all a part of the Alpha Ceremony, another one of our shifter rituals. When Jack challenged the last Alpha of the Western Pack and won his position, he was installed as Alpha and—in a ceremony that I still don't understand—given the identity of his fated mate. Each pack needs an Alpha couple, which means that their Alpha needs his mate. I was Jack's, and that was that.

As an omega, it wasn't as if the other males in my former pack were lining up to mate me even before I met him. They treated me as if I was made of porcelain. Coddled. Protected. I was breakable, and none of the males wanted to be the one to damage the precious omega in their midst.

Since then, Jack has delighted in doing exactly that. But just like how he's the only one who can hurt me, he's *definitely* the only one who can fuck me.

Too bad his Beta didn't get the memo.

From the moment Scott appeared on my doorstep, I knew precisely why he was there. He came on the pretense that he was checking up on his Alpha's mate and pup while he was away, but Scott made it a point to tell me that Jack wouldn't be back until morning. And, wouldn't you know, he was more than willing to stay over the night to make sure we were taken care of.

And if I wanted to invite him to my bed, no one ever needed to know. After all, the full moon is coming, and we're wolves.

We fight.

We fuck.

And Jack would kill Scott if I even thought about accepting his offer.

I sent him away. Of course I did. Even if I had any intention of letting another male touch me, it would never be an arrogant Beta who reminded me of Jack. And it had to be pure arrogance since he not only thought I'd accept him, but he seemed sure that Jack wouldn't pop his head off like a freaking dandelion for attempting to sleep with *his* mate.

The bond between us is weaker than it should be between fated mates, but it's still there. No matter how many times I desperately hope it will break, I know it won't. Not unless Jack wills it to—or until I finally find the nerve to reject him. Since I haven't, choosing any other male while I'm still his fated mate just can't happen.

Of course, the rules don't apply to him. Oh, no. Jack can have countless females, but me? I belong to the Wicked Wolf and him alone.

That's how it's been for three long years so far, and no matter how I wish things were different, I can't see how they're going to change any time soon.

At least I still have Ruby.

I'd do anything for her.

And I mean *anything*.

3

For all the darkness inside of him, Jack's appearance is stunningly bright. A movie-star handsome male with tanned skin, a dent in his chin, and wavy blond hair, he has the build of a California surfer and an air of danger that makes him too, too attractive.

I remember being floored the first time I saw him, and when his lips curved slowly as he looked me over, I couldn't believe my good luck to be his fated mate.

And then I met his eyes.

Jack has eyes of molten gold, but even when he was trying to convince my parents that his reputation was blown out of proportion, that he would be a strong and devoted mate to me—the first of many lies he told me —I noticed that something was stirring in those brilliant eyes.

It wasn't long before I learned that it was evil. Pure and simple. His good looks are just another tool he mastered to manipulate, like his claws and his fangs. The Wicked Wolf of the West has earned every inch of his reputation, and that was back when he was only an alpha shifter. Once he took over the Western Pack as *the* Alpha, he was free to be the vicious, sociopathic wolf he truly is.

Still, as he lets himself into my cabin the night of his return, I can't help but be stricken again by his beauty.

My pup looks so much like him. With her blonde curls and eyes of honey gold, Ruby is the spitting image of her father. Her good heart is all me, though, and I'd much rather her take after me in personality than have her match my appearance. So what if I'm dark where she's fair, that I'm a brunette instead? There's only good when I peer into her eyes, and I'm grateful for it.

I knew as soon as he returned to the Wolf District. The pack sentries howled to him in welcome—okay, in *obeisance*—but even without their howls echoing all the way to my cabin, I felt the tug on our fledgling bond and could sense him.

Tomorrow is the full moon. I hoped he would work off his need with any of his other girls, but he'd hardly been back on our territory when my door is flinging open, Jack looming in my doorway.

Hope for the best, prepare for the worst. It's the motto I live by. So even though I hoped he'd go to any other cabin, I assumed he'd head for mine. I already sent Ruby to her room, tucking my pup into bed a few moments before he arrived.

I struggle to bring a welcoming grin to my face. I've learned that he takes offense if I don't, and if I can avoid setting him off this close to the full moon, I have to.

"Jack. Hi. How was your meet?"

He slams the door shut behind him. "Fuck the meet."

Oh, boy.

That... can't be good.

He lifts his human nose, flaring his nostrils. I can only guess what scent he's picked up on when his eyes seem to flash in recognition.

Uh oh.

I gulp. "Is something wrong?"

"I'd fucking say so. I smell Scott in here."

I don't deny it. I don't even get a chance to before Jack is stalking toward me, a deceptively casual expression on his handsome face as he says, "Heard from some of my wolves that he stopped by last night, but I didn't give him the order to. So, tell me, Janelle. Why was my Beta sniffing around you?"

"He wasn't—"

I'm always so amazed by how fast he is. A man of

that size shouldn't be able to move that quickly, that easily, but before I can finish my sentence, he's in front of me, already swinging his arm up at me.

Jack uses the flat of his hand to strike me in my face. He always says it's because it tempers his strength so I only get knocked around just enough when I "deserve" it, but I know better. With his claws out, they tear into my cheek before his hit sends me flying into the wall nearest to me.

Another mark, I think dazedly as I crumple up on the floor. Forever another mark from my mate.

I watch as his boots appear in my line of vision. He grabs me by my upper arm, wrenching me so that I'm on my feet again. With a rough shake, he snarls, "Don't lie to me, Janelle," before he pushes me back into the wall.

This time, I stay standing.

His icily calm facade was just that, I realize now. It's hiding the blazing fury of a temper that Jack is struggling to control. That first strike was a warning. If I push him, it'll only get worse for me.

Yesterday, I thought to myself that, if I accepted Scott's blatant invitation, Jack would kill him. This close, with my cheek on fire and my shoulder throbbing, I have to admit that I underestimated him.

Right now, I'm not so sure he's not going to kill *me*.

"Jack." I gasp out his name. "I don't know what you think happened, but I told him to leave."

"Did you?" His voice lowers, going so cold that I can't help but shiver. "Was that before or after you gave him a sample of what's mine?"

"I didn't," I swear. "You have to know I didn't. I... ask Scott! He'll tell you that I sent him right away. Please, Jack. Go ask him."

"I would, but he's in no state to answer me." A hollow laugh. "Kinda hard to speak when you're missing your throat."

Oh, Luna, *no*.

Later, I'll look back and recognize that everything went to hell at that very moment. I was so shocked and distraught at how easily Jack admitted to murdering his latest Beta for coming onto me that, for a heartbeat, I slip up. Fear rushes through me, and that stark terror travels straight through the bonds I share with my mate and my pup.

Jack moans at the flavor of my fear. I've heard him murmur in my ear before that it's his favorite, that it's fucking *delicious*, and his eyes go molten as it slams into him.

But my fear does something else to my pup. Breaking the hold I have on her, my little wolf suddenly appears in the front room of the cabin. I don't even know how, considering I closed the door to her room behind me, but there she is and before I could try to retain control over the situation, she's inserted her small body between me and Jack.

Ruby's ears go back. She's showing her teeth to her father, haunches raised as she assumes a defensive position.

My pup is protecting me—*in front of Jack.*

No. No, no, no.

I've done everything I could to hide the truth from my mate. Over the last year, on the few occasions when he would look at Ruby with a suspicious gleam in his gold-colored eyes, I did whatever I had to to distract him.

I would stick my ass out at him. He could never resist that. I'd go on my knees. All fours. He was always a beast in rut, and if my meek nature didn't piss him off enough that he lashed out, then being his bitch would snare his attention away from my pup.

More than that, I used my omega nature to fool him. Not only did I conceal Ruby's alpha aura from him by covering it with mine, but I played the part he expected of one of my kind. He thought omegas were weak? I gave him weak. I gave him gentle. I never fought back, and except for when it came to his mark, I never said no.

I never gave him any idea that I was less than loyal. Devoted. *His.*

And now, as Ruby challenges her alpha father without a hint of fear, he's finally looking at her as if things aren't what he thought they were.

"What's this?" he asks softly. It's not as cold as his

earlier demand and, somehow, that scares me more. "What else have you been hiding from me, my mate?"

Ruby is still growling at him. I click my tongue, catching her attention. Though she's smart enough to know that she shouldn't take her eyes off of the bigger threat in front of her, she's still my baby girl. Her head whips around, searching for me.

"Bed, Ruby girl," I whisper. "Mama says go to bed."

She hesitates, her small wolfish head swinging back to look at Jack again.

"Go," he barks.

Ruby bolts from the room so quickly, her paws can't keep up with her speed. She trips, rolling over herself before she's back on all fours again. I sense her retreating to her bedroom, and though I can't risk walking away from Jack to shut her door, I tell myself it wouldn't do any good anyway. She got out before. My little Houdini would just find another way to escape.

For now, she's out of the line of fire. It's better than nothing.

And that's when Jack says in a loaded tone, "Keep them."

I look over at him. I didn't even notice that I was staring after Ruby until Jack made his demand. After what just happened, I don't know what I expected him to say first, but it wasn't *that*.

Actually, I have no idea *what* he's talking about. "Keep what?"

Blood glistens on the tips of his claws as he points. *My* blood. "The marks on your face. Keep them, Janelle."

Oh.

My fingers lift up to my cheek, tips ghosting against the ruined skin. I'm not sure how since my face feels like it's on fire, but I kind of forgot about the slash marks there.

He didn't.

A small smile curves his lips as he continues to point. "You will wear my mark on your face just like that. Every fucking male will know you belong to me, just like that little bitch is from my seed."

What?

No.

"Jack, I—"

"And if you heal them..." His smile widens. "If they're gone when I come to fuck you next, you'll regret it. I've told you before, Janelle. No one comes between me and my mate, not even your spawn."

He doesn't need to specify his threats. If he says I'll regret it, then I will. He'll do something to Ruby, even though she's as much his pup as she is mine. Because it'll hurt me, and because he knows that *I'*ll do anything to protect my daughter from his cruelty—even keep his marks.

It's all he's ever wanted. Whether he bound me to him

or not isn't really the issue because being marked by Jack is the one thing I've always refused to give him. Now? Now he's leaving me no choice and we both know it.

Jack moves into me. Unlike before, his steps are slow. Purposeful. He *wants* me to see his approach as he says, "Tell me you love me."

He does this sometimes. It's another thing he gets off on, another way to prove he has all the power. I've told him a hundred times. In the three years that I've been *his*, he's never said the same.

I don't think Jack loves anyone but himself. Not me. Not any of his girls. Especially not our daughter.

But I know better than to refuse, especially after that too calm ultimatum.

"I love you, Jack."

"More than anyone?"

"More than everyone."

"More than the bitch?"

My inner wolf wants to lash at him for how he keeps referring to her pup as a bitch.

Lie, Janelle.

"Yes."

He grabs me by my hair. Wrapping the length around his fist, he tilts my head back far enough that I'm forced to stare into his blazing gold eyes.

The tilt becomes a *yank*. I gasp, and my bastard mate takes advantage to shove his tongue in my mouth.

It's a kiss so deep, so unwanted, that it's all I can do not to gag.

Right when I'm ready to plead for breath, he bites. Hard.

I whimper.

Letting go of my hair, he snatches my chin, angling my head so that he can run his gaze over the bloody rips in my cheek. I purposely kept them from healing —*keep them*, he said and, if only for a moment, I'm listening—and he rumbles in pleasure when he can tell that he's won.

"Atta girl."

I swallow, but say nothing.

He pinches my chin anyway. "The full moon is tomorrow, Janelle. You will fuck me then, and you will mate me. We will be bonded. For good this time. No other males for you, and I'll give up my females. I won't need them. Not when I have a mate like you."

I'm scared. For me, but mostly for Ruby, I'm fucking *terrified*. And then Jack drops that bomb on me and the only thing I can think to do is squeak out, "Like me?"

"The moon knew what she was doing when she gave you to me," is all Jack says before he does something that scares me even more.

His gaze goes over my head, and he smiles again. There's something in that grin that has me pulling my chin out of his grip, turning to look over my shoulder.

And there's Ruby.

The Wicked Wolf is grinning at Ruby.

My stomach lurches.

He knows.

There's no way he hasn't figured it out. I can sense a smugness coming from Jack that overlays the possessiveness and the anger that was exploding off of him earlier. Not only that, but he's almost... excited.

Of course he is. After a year of hiding Ruby's true nature from him—after three years of keeping from becoming his bonded mate—Jack believes that he has everything he needs to be the most powerful Alpha in reach. He has the only female alpha as his daughter, and the perfect leverage to get me to bond to him irrevocably.

Unless I leave.

I could. On some of the roughest nights, I would lie awake and think about all the ways I could escape the Wolf District; after Ruby was born, the fantasies developed an urgency even if I admitted that Jack would never let me go. So what if he thought she was an omega? She was still as much his as I was, and he'd do anything to keep us trapped here. There was no point in trying to leave if, in the end, all I'd do was piss him off.

Now? I'm the only thing standing between my vicious mate and my vulnerable pup. Even if being Jack's prisoner is inevitable, it's still my choice. My decision. A mate has to choose, and if I disobey him, if

I heal his marks, I might be able to buy some time to figure out another plan to save my girl from her father.

Jack is an alpha. His rank comes with its own abilities, but empathy isn't one of them—and not just because he's twisted and broken deep inside. He doesn't need to be able to sense my emotions to know what I'm thinking. His ironclad control over the pack —control over *me*—is enough to give him some insight into my chaotic plotting.

Or maybe it's the way that I'm trembling in fear, pure desperation eking out of my pores as I watch Ruby lower herself into another defensive position.

She's going to try to protect me again. I need to calm down. She's reacting to my emotions the same way Jack is, only she wants to save me from them instead of *enjoying* how distraught I am.

He laughs. It's a low chuckle that only makes his next threat all the more chilling.

"I know what you're thinking, my mate. Don't. Because if you even think of refusing me tomorrow, I'll drown the bitch."

He wants a reaction? He gets one.

Whirling back on Jack, I gasp. "You wouldn't."

"Wouldn't I?" His golden eyes glitter brutally. "Oh, Janelle. You know me better than that."

He's right. I do.

"She's just a child!"

"And? She's mine." Jack lashes out his paw, wrapping his claws around my neck before yanking me toward him again. "Just like you are."

The points of his claws slice easily through my skin. I freeze so that they don't go any deeper.

I'm pinned. Just like always with this male, I'm *trapped*.

He slowly lowers his head—but he doesn't kiss me this time. *No*. Instead, he darts out his tongue, gathering up the blood that spilled down my cheek, dripping to pool against my collarbone.

Another guttural moan, then he pushes me away from him. His claws rip through the side of my throat, adding more blood to the pool he just lapped up, but I barely notice.

I lose my footing, but recover in time to turn and swoop Ruby up before she can launch herself at her father.

He laughs again. The light-hearted sound only adds to my terror, and I cling to Ruby for comfort almost as much as to shield her from him and his threats.

As Jack reminds me one final time that he expects to see his marks turned to scars when he comes back during the full moon, all I can hear is the repeated refrain of two words beating against my skull:

Leave, Janelle.

Leave.

Janelle, leave.

Leave—

The spell is broken as soon as he slams the door closed behind him. For the moment, at least, we're alone.

Stumbling backward, clutching my daughter tightly, I sink down on the couch.

I have to leave. And maybe it's a death wish, maybe I'm putting both of us at risk, but I can't sit here and wait until my fate is sealed tomorrow.

He threatened to bond me to him against my will. He promised he'd drown my pup if I didn't.

Who's to say that he wouldn't do that anyway the next time I pissed him off?

I can't stay. I *can't.*

We can't.

We have to leave, and if we fail, at least I can say I tried.

For Ruby's sake, I have to *try*.

4

L eaving is actually far easier than I thought it would be.

Jack isn't just arrogant. He underestimates how dangerous a mother wolf can be when she's backed in a corner and she has her pup to protect. So even though he's given me every reason to go, he doesn't even have one of his wolves watching my cabin after he heads out.

I try not to think about Scott, how only last night he was stopping by to "check up on us". He was a lecherous asshole, but he didn't deserve what Jack did to him. Sure, he challenged Jack as pack leader by making moves on me when Jack was out of the District, but he was his Beta. That should've given him some leeway, right?

I guess not.

Maybe that's why no one's out there. Whenever the next Beta is forced out of the role—one way or another—Jack has to gather his loyal wolves close. He'll have to assure them that the missing wolf had it coming, and even though they know Jack's gone through more Betas than I can count in the three-plus years that he's been Alpha, a few of those lunkheads will still volunteer to be his right-hand wolf.

Plus, the full moon is so close. She'll be affecting the rest of the pack, too, and I can just imagine half of Jack's sentries sneaking off to work out some of their aggression and need. Localized fights will erupt, or the males will either go home to their mates or to whatever single female will have them. Some of the young pups will be getting ready to shift for the first time and happy, content families will be celebrating.

For tonight, at least, no one's thinking about me.

The only one who might be is Jack. But after three years of doing his bidding, of jumping whenever he told me to, of catering to his every need... after three years of being the omega I am, he'll never guess that his visit will have finally spurred me to do something about our broken mating.

Jack doesn't bluff. If he says I'll regret refusing him... if he pointedly promises to drown my pup... I know he means it. No one will stop him, either—no one, except for me. I have no illusions that my escape attempt is going to be successful, but I know I have to try.

For Ruby's sake, if nothing else.

He could threaten me and I'd never react. But threaten my child?

I'm an omega, but I'm still a wolf. My claws are out.

Just in case, I take nothing with me except for a few human dollars and my pup. In the Wolf District, we don't use money. We're kept remote from the rest of the human world, with Jack refusing to mingle with them. Ours is a shifter-only community, where we live side by side and provide for each other. As his mate, I was given everything I needed, but I still had some money that my parents gave me when I first headed west with Jack. I never used it, and though he ordered me to get rid of it, I squirreled it away in one of the first acts of disobedience against my new mate.

I'm glad I did. It's not much, but it's something in case I have to rely on human help to escape. I'm not above using the non-supe creatures, mainly because my home pack had a working relationship with a local human neighborhood. It's pretty rare for shifters to mingle with humans—and almost unheard of for my kind to have anything to do with our sworn enemies, the vampires—but I have no problem doing it, especially since it'll be the last thing Jack expects.

I didn't dare take anything else. Just in case Jack stops back, or one of his runners do, I don't want to draw attention to the fact that I left. At first glimpse, it would seem as if I took Ruby out for a walk. By the time they realize that I've abandoned the cabin, I want to be far enough away that Jack decides it's not worth chasing after me.

Please, Luna. Please make it so that he lets me go...

For the first leg of my escape, I convince myself that maybe I have a chance. I'm going in my skin, the money tucked securely in a pouch around my neck; it's charmed so that, should I shift, I'll still wear it as a wolf even if my clothes are toast. Ruby is wide awake despite the late hour, and the nearly full moon reflects in her curious eyes. She's as quiet as the grave, though. No yips. No whines. As if she can tell that this is extremely serious, she keeps her pudgy arms wrapped tightly around my neck as I walk further and further away from the District.

I waited until it was dark out only because I was hoping that my other packmates would be too busy beneath the moon to notice I was gone. It's a calculated risk, especially since it takes everything I have to fight her pull back toward Jack, but I do. Every time I falter, I glance down at my daughter and push on.

There's a thicket of trees that surround my cabin. Past the thicket is a deep gulley that I can jump easily in my fur. It's a little tricky in my skin, especially with such precious cargo, but I want it bad enough. I just manage to clear the five-foot crevice, then pick up the pace as I disappear deeper into the next densely forested patch of land that hides the District out of sight from the humans.

As a shifter, I can sense the outer reaches of our territory; it's almost like an invisible line that marks all the space on one side as Western Pack land. Go past it and my layer of protection disappears.

Poof. It's gone.

Out there, I'll be considered a lone wolf if I refuse to return to my pack, and if I cross into another pack's territory, I'll be a stranger—and a target.

That's why I planned to hide in a human city instead. Running into another wolf could be just as dangerous as staying behind. Outside of the district, I have my status as the Wicked Wolf's mate working against me, plus the truth of my pup's ranking. Leaving Jack doesn't mean I'm automatically safe, especially since there's always the chance that another enterprising wolf might decide to make a deal with Jack to return me to him.

I try desperately to shake off that thought. Right now, the only thing I need to worry about is escaping Jack's territory. I'll deal with how I'm going to stay away once I've gotten out.

About five miles separate my cabin from the furthest reaches of the Wolf District. My heart is racing, my ears picking up every single sound over my feverish breathing, but I start to feel a little hopeful that I can really pull this off when I've reached about mile four.

And that's when I hear the first howl.

I freeze.

No.

Ruby clutches at the top of my shoulders. "Mama?"

Swallowing back the lump of fear that's suddenly lodged in my throat, I give her a shaky grin. "It's okay, baby. Just... hold tight. Hold tight to Mama. We're gonna run."

Beneath the moonlight, I see her tiny forehead scrunch up. "Wolf?"

She wants to know if she should shift.

I shake my head. "In a little bit. Okay?"

She nods and does what I told her to. She tightens her grip on me and, once I can move past the terror that has me locked into place, I take off at a sprint.

I'm prepared for the next round of howls. It's another packmate, though I'm not sure who. It doesn't matter. Two distinct howls mean two distinct hunters are coming after me.

Because I'm not *that* naive. Wolves are often silent hunters, using howls to communicate with the rest of the pack. This close, and from the pitch of their howl, there's no way that they're not coming after me. Worse, because they're obviously shifters, that howl was on purpose. They *want* me to know I'm their prey.

My one saving grace is that it isn't Jack. I know the

sound of his howl all the way down to my bones. If he's out there, he's being quiet, especially when a third howl—much closer this time—lights a fire under my ass.

One mile. I have one mile to some semblance of freedom.

I'd make it faster if I could shift. Without Ruby clinging to me, I would've. But despite how advanced she is, she's still a pup. It would be too easy for us to separate if she was running alongside me, and I'd be slowed down if I carried her between my fangs. Staying in our skin is a gamble, but I'd rather be caught by Jack's wolves than risk losing Ruby in the woods.

Cradling her head, I hold her to me as I push through the bushes, the trees, past the rocks, and over the fallen logs that act as a natural deterrent to any fool encroaching on pack land. I don't look behind me because I don't want to see the flashing shifter's eyes chasing us. After that last howl, the hunters go silent, but I know they haven't given up.

In fact, I'm pretty sure they're herding me right where they want me.

I didn't forget what marks the end of Western Pack territory. The river is more than thirty feet across and there aren't any bridges nearby. It has rapids dotting along the twelve-mile length, plus a current that makes it super dangerous to try to cross even when you're not desperately clutching your child.

I'm almost positive that they'll expect me to reach the river and stop. I'm an omega, after all, and they'd never guess I'd brave the river.

But I didn't forget. I knew where I was heading all along. If I want to really leave Jack, this is the only way to do it.

I can scent the water in the air as we get nearer to it. It has a few natural smells that call out to my wolf: it's fishy, it's musky, it's *wet*. My hearing might not be as keen as an alpha's, but I pick up on the rushing water before I reach it. I know it's there.

If we want to avoid Jack's wolves, there's only one choice.

Rubbing Ruby's back, I murmur softly, "Shift, baby girl. Come on, sweetie. Shift for Mama."

It'll be easier if we go in our fur. I'm a much stronger swimmer when I'm my wolf, and I'm hoping that it'll be the same for Ruby.

I hate that we have to abandon our clothes so soon. I'd had the idea that we'd make it to the river, strip, and I could find a way to carry them across the raging waters with us. Now I can't even justify the few seconds it'll take to undress.

Ruby's confusion pings off of me. Ever since she could shift, I made sure to teach her not to ruin her clothes, and here I am now, telling her to shift without encouraging her to save her clothes.

"It's okay," I tell her. Then, setting her down, I show her that it is by shifting first.

My clothes explode into tatters, raining down on us both.

Ruby laughs. It's such a sound of delight that, for a moment, I can almost forget about the wolves at our heels. I bark out a laugh of my own before nuzzling her in the side with my damp snout.

Come on, Ruby. Come on—

I let out a huff of relief when my bouncing baby shifts into an excitable blonde pup. She bounds over to the edge of the river. It's like it's all a game to her, and I'm glad. I don't want my girl to be afraid.

I'm scared enough for the both of us.

ALL I CAN SAY IS THANK THE LUNA FOR ALL THE TIMES I used to go swimming back home.

I used my front paw to get rid of as many pieces of our ripped and torn clothing as I could before I said a prayer to the Luna, snagged Ruby by her scruff, and leaped into the icy river.

The current immediately picked us up in its grip. I didn't fight it. As quickly as it moved, it carried us further downstream than I could've run with my pup. Plus, it helped me cover our scent trail. The wolves tracking us would follow our scents to the point where we shifted, but other than knowing that we jumped into the river, they'd have no idea where we went next.

For all they knew, we could've drowned. Jack's threat was a taunt the entire time I let the current sweep us away. Had I doomed Ruby to the same fate I was so determined to avoid? For a few terrifying seconds there, I was almost sure that I had.

Luckily, I didn't. I saved my energy until I judged that we'd made it far enough, then I started to cross the river. I kept worrying that I would lose her and I probably overcompensated by biting down hard on her scruff, but my girl's a trooper. She hung limply from my muzzle, making it as easy as possible for me to push through the water.

The second I finally dragged her out of the river, I know we've crossed out of Jack's territory. The river marks the edge of the Wolf District, and though I've never gone this way before, it ruffles my fur as we leave it behind.

To my surprise, though, we almost immediately pass onto land that belongs to another pack.

Ruby can sense it, too. Even though I'm carrying my pup by her scruff, she whines softly. It's like an electric charge between one step and the next. The air is different. Thicker. More oppressive. My wolf begins to echo Ruby's whine, but I clamp my muzzle shut before it does.

Huh. I had no idea that the Wolf District backed up

directly onto another pack's territory.

I should've guessed. For as long as I've known Jack, growing his pack in size hasn't been his only obsession; more than anything else, he wants to lord over a huge territory. He wouldn't have stopped pushing the edge of his borders unless he was forced to.

Like, oh, bumping up against the border of the nearest pack before trying to shove them away?

This... this makes things a lot more difficult. As much as I want to avoid other shifters until I'm certain I'm free of him, that seems impossible now—and I'm too tired to even think of an alternative plan.

As it is, I've already allowed my wolf to take over. The human side of me is so beaten down by everything that has happened today. I want to collapse, but my wolf's survival instinct is so much stronger. Giving complete control over to her—I'd trust no one else with my pup's safety—I don't put up a struggle when she veers toward the nearest patch of woods instead of trying to find another way out.

My hackles do go up a bit when I sense another shifter not too far from where we are. It's a wolf, like me, and I'm pretty sure it's a male. I pull up short when I catch his scent, but my wolf tugs against my sudden nerves until I remember that I'm letting her lead.

I never should have doubted her. Using the moonlight to guide us, she brings us to a massive stone structure that looks like it's been picked up by a giant, then dropped haphazardly in the middle of the woods. At first glance, I can't tell if it's man-made or natural, but then I notice that it's deeper than it initially appeared. Taller, too.

Not a mountain, not quite, but close enough. A rocky hill? Maybe. I don't really care what it is. It's *safe*. There's a worn-down footpath that leads out of the dense overgrowth of the wooded area, and as my wolf heads right to it as if she'd planned this all along, I realize what she's found.

A cave.

Cavern.

Whatever.

It's somewhere to hide, and though I can scent territory markings all over the rock, the stink of urine is old. No one has been here in a while. I don't have to worry about true animal predators hanging around, either, since the markings would've been enough to warn them away.

If this was any other situation, they would've been enough to warn me away, too.

But not tonight. Not when I finally escaped with Ruby, and not when I've already been chased by Jack's wolves. The panicked swim through the river sapped the last of my adrenaline. I need somewhere safe to hide my pup and get a few hours of rest before I decide what I'm going to do next.

This will have to do.

5

I enter the cave as cautiously as my other half will let me. She assures me that the worst I have to fear is a few chirping insects and maybe a frog or two, but I have to see for myself.

Only when I've proved that it's as safe a sanctuary as I could hope for do I finally loosen my death grip on my daughter's scruff.

She drops to the stony ground before immediately spinning around, ducking under my front legs.

I rumble, letting her know that I'm here. I'm with her.

We're together.

Thank the Luna.

Unfortunately, though, my wolf's fur is still soaked. Hers too. We have no human clothes so, for now, we'll have to stay in our fur. Despite it being summertime, the shadowed cave is chilly. Even if we're drenched, we'll be warmer wearing our fur over being naked in the dark.

I lay down on the ground, nudging Ruby so that she's nestled in front of me while I get as comfortable as I can. Then, once I have, I nod at the space I've left for her. With another of her yips, she plops down between my paws.

She's gotta be exhausted.

Laying one of my paws on her back, I start to clean her with the flat of my tongue. Not the type of bath I prefer to give my girl, but it's all I can do right now.

When she's as dry and as clean as I can make her, she curls up, resting her muzzle on her own paws as she blinks sleepily up at me.

Ah, sweetie.

My girl.

My Ruby—

No.

No.

I don't know why it's only just hitting me now, but as my wolf nuzzles the top of her head, I realize that leaving the Wolf District... that was only the beginning. Sure, we made it out of Jack's territory and onto some other pack's land, but the shifter world is small. There's no way I can hide from Jack forever—I accepted that even before I left the cabin behind—but she, at least, has a *chance.*

If I want to save her from Jack, Ruby Walker the omega wolf has to disappear.

She's too young to know what we're running from, what we're leaving behind, and in some ways, that's a blessing. Maybe we can start over after all. And even if *we* can't, I'll do anything to give her that chance.

It's a good thing that I was always so careful to keep her hidden. The pack knew we had a pup, but Jack didn't push me to show her off to them. She was his dirty little secret, the runt of an omega wolf that he couldn't believe he had sired.

And if Jack had actually sired an alpha?

Oopsie...

I peer down at my daughter. Now that he knows the truth, it's not just me he won't want to get away. I can't even begin to imagine how valuable my little alpha is, and I've had the last year to come to grips with it.

The thing is, *I* don't have to go back there. Getting out was the hard part, but since we never actually bonded, I can leave him; as much as Jack will fume over it, I'm not on his territory so I'm not under his control anymore. He can't bring me back if I don't want to go. But Ruby is still his daughter. He has a claim to her. He's her father, and even though she's here with me, there isn't a single shifter alive that would stop Jack from getting to his daughter.

Which means that, from this moment on, she can't be.

Okay. *Okay.* If she can't be Ruby Walker, who can she be?

When I was pregnant with her, I used to daydream about what it would be like once my daughter was born. There was a connection between us from the beginning, and even if I couldn't tell that she would be so unique, I always knew she'd be my girl.

Ruby was one of my top choices for her name. I had a few others, too, but I was the only one coming up with girl names. Jack was so proud that I was having his pup that he refused to accept that she'd be anything but his Junior.

Of course, then he discovered that she was female and he lost his Luna damned mind over it as if I did it on purpose. He refused to even meet her the first few days of her life, and when he finally did, he just called her "that". Better than "little bitch", but any illusions I had that being a father might change him died a quick death that day.

On the plus side, I got to name her.

And now, a year later, I'm going to change it.

I need something sweet. Something delicate. A name so harmless, no one will ever guess she's a female alpha or the daughter of the Wicked Wolf.

It hits me right as my head starts to feel heavy and I'm ready to follow my dozing daughter into sleep.

Gemma.

My second choice for a name, and due to Jack's refusal to discuss any female names, no one would ever know except for me.

And not just Gemma. To distance her from her infamous father, I also need to change her last name. As soon as Jack took me as his mate, mine was changed to Walker to match his, but even if I gave her my maiden name, it would be too easy to tie her back to me. She has to be someone else entirely.

Gentle.

Non-threatening.

The opposite of a predator—

Swann.

I'm going to call her Gemma Swann.

Who can be afraid of a smiling, blonde pup called Gemma Swann?

But, most importantly, she'll still be my Ruby deep down.

My precious, precious Gem.

GEMMA IS CURLED UP, FAST ASLEEP. I WAITED FOR HER to settle down completely before allowing myself to get a little rest.

And a little is all I get.

Actually, it seems like it's been no time at all when

my wolf suddenly jerks awake, muzzle curled back to show off my fangs as I hurry to all four paws.

When I went to sleep in the depths of the cave, the scent of other wolves was faint. Old. Not any longer. That same male scent from before is more powerful, as if he's followed our scent trail and tracked us to the cave.

The barely audible *click*, *click*, *click*ing of claws against the stone outside just proves it.

Intruder. It's an intruder.

I don't know who exactly is outside of the cave. I don't know why they've decided to track us here; whether they're searching for us on purpose, or if they're just curious about a strange shifter on their territory. I don't *care*. My pup is in the cave which means that I have to do whatever I can to keep everybody else out.

The same urge to protect has me and my wolf going absolutely single-minded.

Protect the pup.

Protect Gem.

I burst out of the cave like a bat out of hell. It could be Jack himself out there and that wouldn't stop me. I'm willing to attack first and make apologies later if I have to.

I've never gone feral before, though I've heard stories of wolves who sacrificed the little humanity they had in order to go full wolf. Is that what's happening now? Could be. I'm running on pure instinct as I leap at the wolf-shaped shadow that is pacing outside of the cave.

He wasn't expecting me to attack. That much is obvious. The male is a large grey wolf, his fur tinged with black on the end, and he's at least twice my size. My omega side screams *alpha*, but it's too late. I'm snapping my jaws, using my smaller size to my advantage.

I go right for his leg. My wolf's fangs wouldn't be enough to do any real damage to his thick throat, but if I can bite through the meat on his back leg, I might be able to catch him off guard.

I do better than that. Because the big wolf wasn't prepared for me to streak out of the cave and snap my jaws on his hind leg, he doesn't hold his ground. Between my hit, my momentum, and the bite, he steps back, losing his footing before he tumbles down the side of the rocky hill.

And because *I* wasn't prepared to knock him off the hill, I clamp my teeth and tumble with him.

I bounce down the side like a freaking pinball, landing on top of the male wolf when we eventually hit the ground below. I can taste the tang of his blood in my mouth, my canines buried deep in the muscle of his leg. I never let go as I fell, but as soon as it sinks in that I'm down here and my baby is back in the cave alone, I quickly react.

Tearing my teeth from the wolf's leg, I jump up. The male wolf shakes off the fall, slowly climbing back to his four legs. Snapping my jaws at him, I warn him against following me before bolting back up to the cave.

Later, when I was thinking more clearly, I couldn't believe that he listened. He had the size—and the aura—of an alpha wolf, and the scent markers I picked up on earlier are mainly his. This part of the woods is definitely his territory. Me and Gem are trespassers... but he doesn't follow me.

At least, not right away.

I give up on sleep. I go back to the cave because I've proven that I can defend it, and Gem needs to sleep. After my run-in with the male, I'm too amped up to even think about doing the same. It's all I *can* do just to drag my pup close to me, placing her between my paws so that my eyes are on her.

A few hours later, the most delectable scent comes wafting past my snout. Like before, my shifter's nose catches my attention first. Only, this time, I'm not geared up to protect my pup.

This is a completely different instinct.

Food. My stomach is grumbling as soon as the scent of fresh meat hits me. There's food out there.

My pup starts sniffing. Her eyes are still closed, but she can smell it, too. A moment later, she lets out a soft whine.

She's gotta be hungry.

That seals it for me.

I pick Gem up by her scruff, padding toward the back of our cave. Until I can figure out what's going on, I want to keep her out of sight. If it's a threat out there, I don't want her getting in the way—or, worse, thinking she has to protect me instead of the other way around.

And if it's not a threat? Just because any other shifter will be able to scent that I'm not alone in the cave, that doesn't mean I have to let them see her.

After I set her down and, with a pointed bark, tell her to stay, I move carefully back to the cave opening. There, laid out like a feast for us, is a deer. I can see the marks where the predator took it down, but the best parts of the kill are left for us to eat.

As a human, I can be pretty picky. When my wolf's in charge? I'll eat anything—but not this.

It smells so good, but when I sniff the carcass, deer isn't the only scent I pick up on. The male who killed it is all over his prey. And, though I can hardly believe it, it belongs to the male wolf that I attacked.

He's left me food. In the shifter world, that has only one meaning. Considering I attacked him, I can't imagine that this is anything other than an attempt at a peace offering, but just in case...

Yeah. I can't eat it, but my pup will starve if I don't let her.

Peering out of the cave, I look for him. His scent

lingers in the air, but I don't see him. The deer is still warm, so I know the kill hasn't been out here long. Still, he's gone.

With a low howl, I call Gemma to me. My pup comes bounding over to me, tongue lolling playfully now that I've let her out of the darkest depths of the cave. Then she sees the deer and begins to flop over in excitement.

I snort out a laugh, swinging my head toward the deer. Gem bumps into my side before diving at the deer's belly.

I'll hunt later. Now I know that there is plenty of prey in these trees, and if the male wolf repaid my attack by leaving a meal for us, I hope he'll look the other way when I go hunting for myself.

Until then, we'll stay right here.

THE DEER IS ONLY THE BEGINNING.

For the next five days, the same male wolf returns twice a day—at dawn and dusk—with a fresh kill. Sometimes it's deer, sometimes it's elk, and after about the third day, he always leaves a hare or two out there.

The appearance of the hares makes me nervous. Though I'm a wolf, I'm not the world's best hunter. Comes from being coddled as a kid, then basically kept as a prisoner. My fight with the male wolf had to be a fluke. I can't take down anything too large, and though it probably takes me three times as long to hunt, I can usually snag a hare to feed myself.

Maybe he thinks they're my preference because he suddenly starts leaving them behind for me. I try to convince myself that his senses are so keen that he knows the type of prey I'm hunting. Otherwise, I have to admit that he's out there watching me while I hunt.

Then again, maybe that's better. If he's watching me, then that means he's not watching Gem...

He has to know I have her with me. I refuse to let my pup leave the cave, just in case, but someone's eating his kills—and it's not me. Still, he brings food every day before disappearing into the trees.

On the sixth day, he doesn't.

Oh, he brings meat. That's not all, though. Next to the kill, there's a bag. I can scent the sugar in the air as soon as I edge out of the cave. Torn between curiosity at what's concealed in there and my insatiable sweet teeth, I don't realize that he's sprawled out on his side near the edge of the footpath until I'm almost all the way outside.

His ears twitch. That's all it takes. His ears twitch, and my head jerks his way. How I missed his scent, I have no idea, and I blame it on how his daily visits keep it current.

The big wolf doesn't get up. He doesn't do more than that simple twitch.

I still turn tail and run back into the cave.

Gem's hungry, though. And I... I really want to know what's in that bag. I wait as long as I can manage, then tiptoe closer again.

He's still there.

It becomes a game of cat and mouse. He's the big bruiser guarding the mousehole, I'm the skittish mouse who can barely pop her head out without worrying that he's going to go for my throat.

But he never does. Every time I check to see if he's gone, he's still laying out on his side, head turned to watch me with his dark gold eyes. Even if I could try to fool myself that he was just a massive grey wolf—and not a shifter—those eyes give him away. He's definitely one of my kind, and his aura just proves that he's an alpha like Jack.

Well, not like Jack. Because this wolf isn't after revenge, and he's being kind instead of cruel.

Maybe that's why his presence out there baffles me as much as it does.

Eventually, my worry for my pup wins out. I don't let Gem go to the mule deer out there, dragging it by its hoof into the mouth of the cave instead.

The wolf doesn't move.

I take heart in that. So, when Gem's eating her fill, I pad softly back onto the ledge.

And... he still doesn't move.

In fact, he seems to be staying as motionless as

possible as if he's trying not to spook me. When I hook my paw around the bag, his eyes seem to light up, and he lets out a soft, huffing sound, but that's all.

I grab the bag between my teeth and high-tail it back inside the cave.

Since leaving Jack, I've stuck to my fur. It's easier to hunt, to bathe in a small creek nearby, to pee. But when it comes to opening up a to-go bag, hands are better than paws. I shift, arching my back to stretch it, then hunch down on the stone floor.

Tearing into the bag, I have to swallow my cry of delight when I discover it's a hefty slice of what has to be strawberry shortcake— complete with whipped cream and a fresh strawberry on top—inside of a plastic container

As a shifter, chocolate can be hit or miss because of the way it historically affects our beasts. Some of us don't mind the eventual headache or the poops, while others get their sugar fix elsewhere. For me, a slice of cake like this is *perfect*.

My hands are filthy. He included a set of plastic utensils but after almost a week of hunting rabbits to fill my belly, I can't be bothered with ripping them open. I just pick up the cake and shove it in my face.

I save a small piece for Gem. The rest? It's demolished in seconds. I even lick the last of the whipped cream from my dirty fingers before wiping my mouth with the back of my hand, then swiping my tongue over that next.

The sugar makes me brave—or maybe I want to let him know that me accepting the cake doesn't change a Luna damned thing. I was weak, so I ate it, but he's still a threat as far as I'm concerned.

But when I go out there to tell him that, he's finally gone.

6

For the next few days, a different slice of cake accompanies his gifted kill.

Lemon cake. Raspberry. Neapolitan. When I eat around the chocolate, he brings me another slice of strawberry shortcake as if I confirmed something for him.

He always waits out there until I take the food. On the tenth day of me living in the cave with Gem, I feed my pup the meat while I leisurely eat the slice of vanilla sponge he left me. When I'm done, I shift back to fur to peek outside—yelp in surprise.

I expected the wolf to be gone. If he wasn't, I expected him to be in his fur.

He's not.

Where the big wolf was lounging on his side before, there's a male in his human form standing there. I don't know where he got the change of clothing from since all wolves go from fur to naked skin, but he's wearing a pair of jeans, a dark grey t-shirt, and no shoes.

He's also one of the most ruggedly handsome males I've ever seen before in my life.

He's tall, his shoulders wide, the sleeves on his tee struggling against his biceps. He has shaggy, sandy brown hair that he's pushed back from his face; I can see the track marks from his claws. His face is long, his jaw sharp, and his nose a little crooked. Unlike my former mate, he's not classically handsome, but I'm momentarily struck dumb anyway.

"Hi, there. Don't be afraid. I just thought maybe it's time to introduce ourselves."

Friendly enough. And his voice, though I can tell he's keeping it low and soothing on purpose, is quite cheerful. I sense no malice or anger coming off of this male, but something about his presence has my nerves flaring up all the same.

Between my yelp and my sudden anxiety, it's no surprise that my protective pup comes barreling out of the cave, rushing to protect me.

Her appearance triggers my instincts. Shaking off the strange hold he has on me, I quickly snatch Gem by the scruff, all but throwing her back inside the cave.

Too late, though. The damage is already done.

I take a few moments to check on my daughter. I

need to calm her; as always, she's my first—my only—priority. Gem nuzzles my front leg, glad to know I'm safe. I do my best to reassure her even as my head spins wildly, not so sure that *she's* safe.

The male saw her. I've spent days trying my best to keep her out of sight, but the cat—well, *wolf*—is definitely out of the bag.

What happens now? I don't know, and after I calm myself a little, I gingerly step back out onto the ledge to see if the male has taken his confirmation and run off.

He hasn't. I guess he's after a little more info because, as soon as he sees me, he immediately asks, "So, is that your pup?"

I should've been expecting the question, but it still rubs my fur the wrong way to hear him ask it in such an interested tone. Gem is mine and no one else's.

In answer, I bare my teeth and snarl.

"Hey, hey there. No offense meant. I was just checking. Can you blame me? I've been wondering who's been in there with you. I thought I saw you carrying a pup that first night, but I wasn't so sure. She's a cutie."

My hackles rise at his compliment. Did I get it wrong? Was the food a gift for Gem and by encouraging her to eat it, I was telling him that she was available?

No, no, no.

Rather than be mollified by his explanation, I'm so furious that I snap my teeth at him.

He holds up his hands. "Ah, Luna. Look, I didn't mean it like that. Does it come out better if I say that she takes after her mom?"

Nope.

If he thought sweet-talking me now is going to make things better, he's *wrong*. I'd pretty much suspected all along that he was trying to make some kind of calculated move on me—that's what the gifting of food means to us shifters, after all—and though I have no idea *why*, it's definitely better than thinking he was after my girl. Doesn't mean I'm interested, no matter what me eating the cakes might signify to him.

To make *my* point, I force my wolf to throw it up.

His eyebrows go sky-high, but instead of getting angry in return, he smiles. A real, honest-to-Luna smile that reaches his dark eyes. "Point taken. At least I hope it tasted good going down." With a nod, he adds, "And, on that note, I'll make sure to bring strawberry shortcake tomorrow. You seem to like that one."

It's my favorite, but I give him no sign that it is.

"'Til tomorrow then. You be safe out here, alright?"

Is that a threat? Maybe coming from someone else, I might take it that way. But—for reasons I don't want to examine too closely—not from this male.

He waves at me, then starts to walk away in his skin. He's only gone a few steps before he turns around, not even a little surprised to see that I've been watching him go.

"Oh. One more thing. Name's Paul." He waits a beat. "Paul Booker." Another nod. "Nice to meet you."

I get the feeling he expects me to know who he is from just his name, but I don't. I have no freaking clue. I'm lucky I knew as many packmates in the Wolf District as I did, let alone any of the neighboring wolves.

In response to his name, I turn around. My pup has started to get curious herself, creeping out of the cave to watch the exchange between her mama wolf and the strange male.

Wonderful. Already my one-year-old thinks she knows better than me.

With a huff, I use my paw to push Gem back into the cave again before following her inside, all while purposely ignoring the way Paul chuckles softly behind us.

TRUE TO HIS WORD, HE'S BACK AS SOON AS THE SUN is up.

I didn't sleep a wink last night. Every time I closed my eyes, I just kept thinking about what his endgame could possibly be. I doubt it is as simple as him being a male interested in the new female in town, but Paul is definitely nothing if not persistent.

He doesn't arrive in his fur. I guess since I didn't

lunge for his throat after he shifted yesterday, he figures that it's safe for him to be in his skin while my wolf is out.

It is. After everything he's done for me over the last week and a half, I feel a bit guilty for the way I treated him the first night. I had no way of knowing that he was a good guy—and I'm still not so sure that I can trust him—but he's been nothing but kind to me and Gem since.

Even so, I pad out carefully when I catch his scent on the early morning breeze.

One good thing about Paul arriving in his skin? He carries a bag in each hand. Stopping at the furthest edge of the upper level of the hill, careful not to test my boundaries, he purposely looks away from me as he busies himself unpacking the bags. There's Tupperware in one, and—as promised—a slice of strawberry shortcake in the other.

He sets the cake down. Lifting up the Tupperware, he peels off the lid, showing me the macaroni and cheese inside.

"Your pup looks young. I asked one of my packmates and they said young pups love this. Thought maybe she might be getting sick of just meat. Here." Paul sets it down, nudging it closer to me with his boot. He's wearing shoes today, a clear sign that he doesn't plan on shifting anytime soon. "Sniff it. If you think it's safe, give it to your girl."

He's right. Mac and cheese is my daughter's absolute favorite when she's in her skin. I still can't figure out his motives, but Gem would love this. Giving it a quick sniff, I can tell that it's exactly what he says it is: noodles, butter, milk, and cheese.

With a jerky motion, I hop behind the Tupperware, using my snout to push it all the way into the cave. For the most part, Gem knows to stay inside when Paul's around, and though she's chomping at the bit to get to those noodles, she waits until I push it in front of her.

She doesn't even pause to shift back. She digs her nose into the Tupperware and starts to gobble it up.

I spare a loving look at my pup, then trot back out to Paul.

While I was feeding Gem, he dared to come a little closer. There are still a good ten feet separating us, but he took advantage of my distraction to move the plate of strawberry shortcake right in front of the cave's opening.

My mouth waters looking at it.

He can tell, too. But instead of rubbing it in my face, he shrugs. "It's just cake. Hardly a meal. Junk food, right? Go on. It's okay."

He's an alpha wolf. I've known that from the beginning. He's an alpha, and though he's not using his dominance against me, I decide to obey him mainly because I really, really want that cake. If he's willing to twist our rituals around so that accepting the cake doesn't mean what it usually does, then there's no reason for me to deny myself.

I eat as daintily as possible while as a wolf, oblivious to the way he watches me nibble and lick until I'm done and I catch him watching me closely.

"Done?" he asks.

I nod.

"Good. I've got a question for you. Please don't hurl if you don't have to, but you seem to be alone with just your pup. Where's your mate?"

I should've known when he requested that I not throw up that I wasn't going to like his question.

I huff, but that's all. It's better than puking, but my bile does come up a bit as I'm suddenly thinking about Jack again.

"He's definitely not here. Is he dead?"

I wish. But since I'm sure that Jack will outlive us all if only out of spite, I shake my head sharply, hoping that he'll get the hint and stop this line of questioning.

"Then, where—"

Know what? I can't do this in my fur. I might have been able to eat the cake as a wolf, but there's one thing I can't do while shifted and that's speak.

He's not going to drop this. I don't know why he's pushing this—and, okay, maybe I do—but I can tell that this is one topic that he wants to know about. Worse, I've been incredibly selfish. He needs to know about Jack if only because odds are that he's going to eventually figure out that this is where I've been hiding.

So, before he finishes his latest question, I shift back.

Paul's jaw clamps shut. His eyes widen, but he quickly looks away.

Of course. I must look like a mess. I've probably got cream in my hair from where it stuck to my fur, and I'm totally naked. Not that that should bother him. In most packs, nudity is just another part of life. So long as there isn't any sexual intent behind it, it's perfectly natural to be wearing your skin and nothing else.

It takes Paul a few minutes before he turns back to look at me. His eyes are still pretty wide, and I can see a hint of a blush staining his cheeks.

I pretend I don't.

Jack. He really needs to know about Jack.

"I had a mate," I confess, "but we never bonded. Not completely. I decided that I deserved better, so I rejected the mating bond." For the most part, at least. "He's not dead, but I wish he was."

Paul's brow furrows. "Do I know him?"

With as widespread as Jack's reputation is, I'd bet on it. Then there's the fact that they're basically *neighbors*...

I almost lie to him. It would be so easy to give him another name, but this close to the Wolf District, it's only a matter of time before my former packmates track me here. This male is a stranger to me, but he's been kind. At the very least, he's kept Gem fed. The least I can do is be honest so he knows exactly why I'm not worth him wasting his time.

"You might. His name is Jack Walker."

"The Wicked Wolf?"

Oh, yeah. He knows.

I nod.

"And the pup? Is that—"

When it comes to my pup, all bets are off. Whatever it takes to protect her, I'll do, starting with telling the curious shifter: "Her name is Gemma Swann."

"Gemma... Swann?"

I know why he's confused. I admitted that Jack is my mate—my rejected mate—so it only follows that she should be his pup. But while I'll stick with Janelle Walker for now, my pup—my ordinary omega pup—is Gemma.

"Yes."

There's no denying the dare in that one word. He could try to pry, he could even use his status to force me to tell the truth, but unless he does, that's all he's getting out of me.

With a nod, he takes my answer as it is. "Okay. What about you?"

"What about me?"

"For almost two weeks now, I've wondered who you are. It isn't often a feral she-wolf breaks into our territory and attacks the first wolf who comes to help her. Of course, I get it. You've got a pup to protect. But we have a pack to protect. So, first, I'd like to know your name."

I've already told him about Jack. I don't see any reason why I shouldn't give him this.

"Janelle. I'm Janelle."

"Will he be coming for you, Janelle?"

It's the same question I've been asking myself on repeat since I left. Will he? Does he care? Or will he never stand to let an omega wolf get away from him?

Again, I want to lie. But I can't.

"I want to believe he won't. But he's the Wicked Wolf of the West."

"So he probably will," Paul adds.

I shrug.

I'll give him credit. He tries so hard not to stare at my boobs as I do.

Then, as if he just remembered something, he goes back to where he left another one of his bags. He opens it up, pulling out a bundle of fabric. It's a pale green color that I adore right away. A color like that suits my dark hair and my hazel eyes, a shade I often wear myself—when I had the pick of my closet, at least.

"Here."

"What?"

"For you. I thought you might like this."

He tosses the bundle of fabric at me. Suspicion wars with curiosity, but the need to see what it is wins out, just like it did with that first slice of cake. I catch it, shaking it out.

It's a simple dress. And, unless I'm imagining it, it's just my size.

I look over at him.

He's blushing again. An alpha male who has to be at least a few years older than my twenty-three, and he's blushing.

"I, uh... I've got a smaller one for your Gemma, too. I wasn't sure you had anything to wear besides your fur."

Oh. So he wasn't looking away because I'm a disaster. From the hint of arousal I can sense coming off of him, his discomfort with my naked body is *definitely* sexual.

Oops. It's been so long that a male saw me as a female and not just a body to fuck that I guess I forgot what it was like. With a mumbled apology, I pull the dress on.

"Oh, good. It fits. Corinne will be glad."

Don't ask, Janelle. You have no reason to wonder—

"Corinne?"

"My sister," Paul explains. "She's the baker who made all the cakes. She's been hounding me to let her meet you, mama wolf to mama wolf, but..."

I don't know whether he meant to do it on purpose

or not, but he glances down at the back of his jean-covered thigh—right where I had bitten him as a wolf.

"Sorry," I whisper.

His head jerks up. An expression I can't quite read flashes across his handsome face before he quickly replaces it with a friendly grin. "You got nothing to be sorry about. I knew what I was risking, sneaking up on you with your pup. No problem. But Corinne's right. She wants me to bring you back to the pack with me. Especially now that I know your ex-mate is a threat, it's not a good idea for you to stay out here on your own."

I know that. I've been trying to work up the nerve to grab Gem and continue on our journey, anything to get us further away from Jack. But the cave was safe and Paul kept bringing us food and, well, I didn't.

Going with him to his pack sounds like a dream come true—if I could trust him.

I want so desperately to trust him.

He can tell that I'm waffling. I haven't had a good night's sleep since I left Jack, and if I was among other shifters, it might be easier to hide Gem than if we stayed on the outskirts of his pack's territory.

Still—

"I don't know."

"What's there to know? You come with me. My pack will keep you safe. I promise."

I want to believe that. But just because Paul and his sister think I should, that doesn't mean that they speak for the whole pack. And if any packmate invited a stranger into the District without Jack's permission, you could be sure that he'd take that as a challenge.

"Shouldn't you ask your Alpha first?"

"Good idea," he agrees easily. *Too* easily. After clearing his throat, he says, "Paul, what do you think? Should we bring a brave female in need and her young pup back to the pack so that she can finally get some food and some rest? And then maybe you won't have to spend everyday trying to convince her we're trustworthy?"

In a slightly different voice, he answers himself. "Why, yes, Paul. I think that's a wonderful idea."

My mouth falls open.

He grins at me. "Okay. Alpha says yes. You ready to go?"

It takes me a moment before I find my voice again. I knew he was an alpha wolf, but—

"You're not just an alpha? You're the Alpha? Of this territory?"

"The Lakeview Pack. And yup. Couldn't you tell?"

After spending so long with Jack, I guess I expected all Alphas to be monsters whether they were in their skin or their fur. But Paul... he's so kind. So thoughtful. Friendly and funny, too.

Also really, really persuasive. It doesn't take much more convincing before I realize that he's right. Now that I know that Paul's the Alpha, I agree to follow him into the heart of the pack territory where I'd be part of a crowd of humans instead of a lone wolf with her pup.

When I give in, Paul hands me the dress for Gemma. It's a miniature version of the one he gave me and I can't help but smile as I hold it.

He starts cleaning up everything he brought with him while I go into the cave. As soon as Gem notices that I'm in my skin, she shifts back. There is yellow cheese sauce *everywhere* and, for some reason, that makes me laugh. Leaning down, I tickle Gem's chest, getting her to squeal with laughter with me.

I already feel so much lighter and we haven't even left the cave yet.

After I tug the dress over Gem's matted curls, I pick her up, propping her on my hip. Swooping down again, I grab the Tupperware, smiling again when I see that my baby licked the whole thing clean.

There will be food in the pack. Running water. A bed.

Bodies between us and Jack...

Yeah. I... really didn't put up much of a fight, did I?

7

Paul is a chatty shifter. He keeps up a steady stream of conversation as he guides us back down the hill. I can sense him resisting the urge to grab my elbow and help me down, and I'm not sure how to take that. He doesn't just grab me, though, and I appreciate it.

He tells me more about his older sister, Corinne, and her twin pups; a pair of rambunctious boys a year older than Gem. I hear about Marcus, his Beta. Miss Patty, an old, crotchety wolf that is the pack's surrogate granny. And on and on and on... it's actually kind of nice, even if I'll probably never get to see any of them.

The Lakeview Pack is definitely smaller than the Western Pack. In the Wolf District, there are at least a hundred and fifty members who live in the immediate territory. In Lakeview, he has about forty packmates and the way he tells it, they're all dying to meet the stranger wolf in their woods.

One thing stands out to me, though. Paul is an Alpha, but if there's one person that he has mentioned yet, it's his mate.

Alphas have mates. It's how it's done. And he mentioned in his chatter that he's been Alpha for two years now. So—

"Will I be meeting your mate, too?"

"No," he says. Before I can ask him why, he adds, "Because I don't have one."

Oh.

That's... unusual.

During the Alpha Ceremony, when a new male is installed as Alpha of the pack, the Luna gives her blessing for his right to rule—and, in my experience, she also passes down the name of the female that will rule at his side as his mate.

It's how I got paired off with Jack, after all. The Luna said I was his fated mate, he came and got me, and that was that.

"How is that possible? Didn't the Luna tell you who she is? Your fated mate, I mean."

"Nope. I'm sure I have one out there somewhere, but I wasn't interested in an arranged mating so I never asked."

I can't believe what I'm hearing. I've never heard

any wolf act so unconcerned when it came to their mate like that.

"But it's fate—"

Out of the corner of his dark gold eyes, he gives me a knowing look. "Are you telling me she always gets it right?"

Considering I've already admitted who my fated mate is, we both know the answer to that.

"The way I see it," Paul adds, "it's pretty simple. I'm the Alpha. Alpha makes rules. Sometimes I decide that an ancient rule is silly and I change it. Forcing me to mate someone just because there's supposed to be an Alpha couple? Silly rule. Changed it. I've always wanted to choose. Now I get to."

As we continue to walk together, I have to admit that I love Paul's outlook on things. I guess, when you are the Alpha, it makes sense to change things around. As an omega, I never would dare, but he isn't wrong. A lot of our traditions and rituals are dated, and maybe if I hadn't put so much stock into the idea of a fated mate, things would've worked out better for me.

So lost in thought over what Paul said, I'm barely paying attention to where we're going. He told me we're going closer to where the pack lives, but when we arrive, I only see one single cabin.

It's huge, too. It has at least two floors and is three times as wide as the cabin I had back in the District.

From the size alone, I know where he's taken me. The fact that it's covered in his scent just confirms it.

This is the Alpha's cabin.

Paul's cabin.

"Home, sweet, home," he says cheerfully. "Come on. Let's get you settled inside."

"What? No! I can't stay here. We can't stay here."

For so many reasons I have to find somewhere else to go. I mean, I was the Alpha's mate for three years and I never once set foot inside of his assigned cabin. Only a bonded mate is allowed to stay in there, and I'm still basically just a hopeless stranger to Paul.

He has to know why I'm refusing. Though he loses his easy smile, he doesn't argue with me.

Instead, he says, "What about the den? There's a bedroom off of it that I save for packmates in need. I don't mean to be pushy or anything... I just want to see you safe."

While the Alpha's cabin is specifically for the Alpha and his mate, there is always one part that's designated as the den. It could be a kitchen, a living room, an office... some space that's welcome to all packmates. Anyone can visit there, even me.

A room off the den?

Yeah.

I can do that.

I DON'T REALIZE HOW BONE-TIRED I AM UNTIL PAUL leaves me and Gemma alone in our new room.

Though all I wanted to do was drop down on the massive bed that took up most of the space, I don't. Instead, the first thing I did was run into the attached bathroom and scrub my hands. Propping Gem up on the sink, I scrub her rosy cheeks and use my claws to try to get most of the tangles out of her curls.

He made sure to tell us that everything in the room and the bathroom is free to all packmates. I hate that it feels like snooping, but he was the one who mentioned diapers first. In her wolf form, Gem doesn't need them. In her skin, she does. There was a closet in the bathroom full of countless toiletries, including five different-sized diapers.

Once I cleaned up my daughter and put her in a diaper, I tucked her into the bed. Paul promised he'd find me a crib if I wanted him to. I wasn't worried about it. I've grown used to sleeping next to my baby and I wasn't sure my wolf could handle a separation so soon after everything that happened.

Gem went right to sleep, her belly full of mac and cheese, her heart content in the knowledge that her mama was near. I thought about taking a shower before deciding to just wipe the dirt off my bare feet so that I didn't feel so grimy, climbing into the clean bed.

After that, I knock right out. I sleep like the dead,

and when I wake up again later that afternoon, my heart nearly stops.

Gem's missing.

My girl is *gone*.

Throwing back the covers, I sniff frantically, trying to track her by scent. Once I have it, I run after it.

In Paul's cabin, the den is part-kitchen, part-dining area. It was like that in my home pack, too. Us shifters are ruled by our appetites, whether it's food or... other things. Most packs congregate where the food is made.

In the Wolf District, there is no den, and that tells you nearly all you need to know about Jack...

My former mate's arrogant face pops into my brain as I think the worst. Gem's gone because he found her, he has her, she's gone.

She's—

She's in the den with Paul.

Gem's wolf is back, and she's playfully gnawing on something that I think—*hope*—is a chicken bone. Paul is sitting cross-legged about a foot away from her, close enough that he can reach her without hovering over her.

She doesn't notice that I'm here. That I'm two seconds away from losing it entirely. Nope. She's too busy with her bone.

Paul notices. As soon as I come racing into the room, feet slapping against the hardwood floor, he lifts his head and smiles.

I want to strangle him.

No, Janelle. Strangling your host is a surefire way to get kicked out of the pack. It's also against my nature, but when it comes to protecting my baby, I've realized there are some things an omega might just do anyway.

"I... Sorry about running in here like this. I woke up and couldn't find my daughter."

He looks down at her. "See? You're getting me in trouble with your mom. I asked you if she knew you were awake and what did you do, Kitten? You shifted so you didn't have to answer me, then stole some of my lunch."

That explains the bone, I guess. And why she was missing from the room. Little Miss Houdini strikes again.

But... *Kitten*?

"Kitten?"

"Uh-huh. I mean, how sure are you that she's a wolf?" Paul runs his fingers through Gem's fur. "She seems more like a Kitten to me."

Honestly, I know he's teasing, but I can't even deny it. My girl preens at his gentle strokes, letting out a soft rumble that, if I didn't know any better, I'd think it *was* a purr.

He glances up, meeting my gaze. "I made chicken wings while you were sleeping. There's still some left in the kitchen."

"Thank you," I say politely, "but I can fend for myself."

I don't have much. Just the few dollars I kept stowed away in my pouch. I had hidden it in the cave my first night inside, grabbing it before I left with Gem and Paul.

"I understand. Anyway, you're welcome to anything in the fridge. Cabinets, too. And if there's something else you want, let me know. There's a human shop a few miles away that doesn't ask too many questions about massive meat orders."

Another thing that's so different from the Wolf District. Jack never relied on human stores. Even if we were in our skin most of the time, he never once let us forget that we were really wolves at heart.

And... I'm thinking about my former mate again.

I shake my head, trying to shove him out of my brain.

Paul frowns. "I understand that you don't want to accept anything from me, but you gotta eat."

Huh?

"Sorry. You're right. I..." How to explain? "I'm just thinking about something. I am hungry, though. Thank you. I'm sure I'll find something."

Nodding, Paul gives Gem one last stroke before taking his hand back. My pup whines, but instead of being annoyed, he barks out a laugh and rubs the top of her head. "I tell ya, Kitten. You're gonna be a heartbreaker." Looking over at me again, he winks. "Just like your mama."

This time, when my heart nearly stops, it has nothing to do with Gem—and everything to do with Paul Booker.

DESPITE HOW EAGER HIS PACKMATES ARE TO WELCOME me and Gem, Paul proves that he really is the Alpha by putting his paw down. For the first few days of our stay, he announces that the den is off-limits. It's clear that he wants us to feel comfortable here, that he's inviting us not just into his cabin, but also his pack.

He's also completely upfront and honest with me when it comes to how seriously he's taking the threat of my former mate—especially since some of his pack enforcers have reported that unfamiliar shifters are testing their borders. Over the last week or so, there have been a couple of sightings, unknown wolves looking for ways to sneak into the territory without being caught, and suddenly Paul's urgency when it came to us moving out of the cave makes a ton more sense.

Jack's looking for us. I'm sure of it. I bet Paul does, too. But instead of treating us like a problem, he bends over backward so that we know we belong.

Because it's not only the threat of Jack that he's

taking seriously. Now that I'm safely tucked away inside of the den, Paul's scent has changed. It's not the slimy, oily lust that had oozed off of Scott, or the heat of Jack's need whenever he thought of rutting, but I've been a mature female long enough to know when a male is attracted to me.

And Paul? He is.

The food had a meaning. I knew it did. In the shifter world, when a male gifts a female food, it's his way of saying that he's a good provider, that he will protect me, he will feed me, and I have nothing to worry about when he's near.

I'm trying desperately to pretend he's only doing this because he's the Alpha. Jack isn't only a contradiction; he's an outlier. Most Alphas are devoted to their pack, seeing each packmate as his to care for instead of his to rule over. From what I can tell, it seems like Paul is one of the good ones. He knows I'm in trouble. While I'm on his land, he'll treat me as one of his own.

That doesn't mean he sees me as his, though.

Right?

Wrong.

Even though I know that he must have plenty of demands on his time, Paul is careful to spend plenty of it tending to me and Gem far more frequently than is called for. I'm so hungry for real, cooked meat that I eat the chicken wings that he offered, pointedly ignoring the pleased look that flashes across his handsome face as I do. Over lunch, he doesn't quite pry, but I find myself confessing more than I planned on.

He's just so Luna damned easy to talk to. And though I've only been talking to him since yesterday, I feel like I know his inner alpha wolf intimately after all those days he came to visit us at the cave. His eyes are darker than Jack's, but they're so much kinder. When I peer into them, I can't help but tell him more than I should.

Like how I ran from my ex-mate the same night that he saw me tearing through his woods. How I'm an omega and so is my daughter; he doesn't contradict me on that point, and I have no reason to believe he doesn't buy my lie. With my cheeks flaming as I look down at my sauce-covered fingers, I even apologize for biting his leg and basically throwing him off the hill.

Paul laughs, telling me not to mention it. Then, grabbing a napkin from the pile on the table, he licks it with his tongue and starts to clean my fingers. His motions are careful yet sure, and he has my wrist cradled in his palm, napkin swiping away the sauce before I even realize what he was going to do.

He's so gentle that it doesn't even occur to me to jerk out of his grasp. I haven't been touched by another male since the first time Jack pushed me to my knees, using his claws to rip my shirt open before he marked my chest the first time.

Bloody and in shock at how he was treating me, my

first time mating was with a cruel, large male shoving himself inside of me. He didn't even pretend to be a thoughtful lover my first time and it only got worse after that.

Paul... Paul's different. In so many ways, he's different. And, okay, I'm skeptical. Of course I am. I can't believe that he's doing this because of *me*. I keep telling myself it's because he's a good guy *and* a good Alpha.

The second night we're in Lakeview, though, I can't pretend any longer.

We eat dinner together. Me, Gem, and Paul. He was busy meeting with Marcus for most of the day so I decided to make myself useful and prepare a meal for him for a change.

Was I aware of how it looked? Yes. Did I know that he'd see me as making a meal for him as the next step in this strange dance we were performing? Yes to that, too.

I... might've been testing him a little. On the very rare times that I ate with Jack, he accepted the food as his due. He wasn't grateful—in fact, he always found something to complain about—but eating my food didn't mean he thought I cared for him. Why would he? I was supposed to be devoted and loyal to him because I was his mate. Nothing changed that.

With Paul, I want to see how he would react. Will he eat first because he's the Alpha and I owe him this?

Or will he refuse it because he doesn't want me to get the wrong idea after all?

Neither, actually. Paul... he *blushes* again. The first time hadn't been a fluke. He blushes, then he thanks me, and we eat together after he insists I take the largest potato when I point-blank tell him that I made the biggest steak for him so it's his instead of mine.

No matter why he's doing it, he's still trying to take care of me. For the first time since I met him, I let him. I eat the freaking potato, and Paul smiles as he cuts into his steak.

When I go to put Gem to bed later that night, Paul asks if I can join him in the kitchen again after I'm done. My pulse picks up at his request, but I nod before carrying my full and dozing pup back to the room where we're still staying.

She goes down easier than I hope. I'm so nervous to find out what it is that Paul wants that I linger at her side of the bed longer than I should. I can sense his alpha aura—not as overwhelming as others, yet still undeniable—pulsing on the other side of the den, waiting for me.

I take a deep breath and, after running my hand over the top of Gem's head, move toward the door.

8

J ust like I thought, Paul has moved toward the edge of the kitchen, as close to where the bedroom is without actually stepping into the dining area.

He gives me a grin as crooked as his nose. "She sleeping?"

"I nod."

"That's good. Rambunctious kitten, she needs her rest when she can get it." Paul likes to call her 'Kitten'. What had surprised me at first has become almost endearing. "She gonna be out long?"

"She sleeps through the night now."

"So she won't miss you if you're gone?"

Where is he going with this? "She can sense if I'm not nearby, but it won't bother her unless it's for an extended period of time. Why?"

"Because, if it's okay with you, I'd like to show you something."

"Paul—"

He holds up his hand. "Hear me out. We won't be gone long. Promise. It's just... the sun's about to set. This is the best time of day for you to see something."

I look him over. His dark gold eyes have lightened with barely concealed excitement, like he really wants me to see whatever it is he has to show me. But his expression is more guarded, as if he's sure I'll politely disagree.

To my surprise—and his—I nod. "Let me grab my shoes."

Since staying here, Paul's provided Gem and me each with an extra dress, a pair of pajamas, and shoes to protect our human feet. I tried to give him my pouch of money to pay for them, but he wouldn't hear of it. Literally. The goofy alpha put his paws over his ears, saying "la, la, la," until I laughed and simply thanked him for his kindness instead.

They're a simple pair of white slip-ons, maybe a size bigger than I need, but they do the job. Paul said there's a small trading station that one of the pack-mates runs once I feel comfortable meeting them. I can pick out fresh underclothes or see if there are some hand-me-downs that fit better, or I could put in a request to one of the wolves who run out to the local human city.

He promises me that, even though I can't see them, there are plenty of his wolf enforcers who will watch the cabin while we're gone. And though I'm an over-protective mama, I want to show him that I believe him. He hasn't given me any reason not to, and if it turns out another Alpha has made a fool out of me... well, I took him down once before, didn't I?

OKAY.

This was worth it.

Logically, I knew that any pack called Lakeview would have some kind of lake. It's in the name after all, and shifters aren't the most creative when it comes to naming their packs. Jack's based on the West Coast; boom, Western Pack. I've heard of the Mountainside Pack in the East that, you guessed it, live on the side of a mountain. The Northern Pack's another one, skirting the border to Canada.

And Lakeview has a grand lake.

Paul wasn't exaggerating when he said that the sunset was the best time of the day to view this sight. As the sun sets over the placid water, it shimmers and shines and turns the pale blue water almost purplish-pink. A few stray clouds reflect in the water.

It's brilliant. Beautiful.

And when I finally rip my gaze from the sight,

turning to see Paul watching me as if he thinks *I'm* brilliant and beautiful, I can't deny the chemistry—and the fledgling bond—sparking between us any longer.

I drop my gaze to the grass, digging the toe of my shoe into the dirt. The more I've been thinking about it, the more I've convinced myself why he's so determined to take care of me.

It's my fault. Omegas are cosseted. Catered to. Adored. And, somehow, by expending so much of my aura to cover Gem and make her appear like another omega, I must've snared this kind-hearted alpha.

I sigh. "You don't have to do this, Paul."

"What?" He sounds confused. "What are you talking about?"

I guess I have to explain.

"I'm not trying to lure you on purpose. I'm an omega. It's instinct that you would want to take care of me, to think you care *for* me, but I swear I'm not doing it on purpose."

"What? Janelle—"

Now, the more I convinced myself that he's only doing this because of the way his type of wolf reacts to mine, the more I realize that there is only one thing I can do. I've already been hiding out on his territory for almost two weeks. Since then, Jack's scouts have been sniffing around, even if they haven't figured out that I'm here yet.

But they will. I know it.

And I can pay Paul back for his kindness by putting him between me and my psycho ex-mate.

"Anyway, I'm glad you showed me this. Your lake. It's... it's gorgeous. I would've been sad to miss it when I go." Because I have to. What else can I do?

"When you go?" he echoes.

His voice has changed. Instead of sounding confused, he sounds too, too quiet. Like this is the last reaction he expected after bringing me here.

It's for the best. "Yes."

"From the den?"

I shake my head.

No. Not from the den.

Paul doesn't say anything to that.

It's awkward now. I still can't bear to look at him, and I'm already kicking myself for how I'm handling things. As an omega, this should be easier than it is. If I can attract him to me, I should be able to break that tie so that he doesn't feel like he *has* to protect me.

"I'm sorry. I didn't mean to drag you into any of this. Maybe I should just grab my baby and go." Yeah. That seems like the best idea. "Thank you, Paul. I... you have no idea how much I appreciate what you've done for me. But... yeah. I should go."

Still avoiding his gaze, I start to hurry away. I've only gone a few steps, though, when his soft voice chases after me.

"Just about two weeks ago, I came across a

wounded she-wolf. She was so feral that, at first, I thought she was a *true* she-wolf."

I hesitate. "I said I was sorry for biting you."

"Why?" There's such a curious note in that one word, it has me jerking my head over my shoulder to glance up at him. "I'm not."

My breath catches in my throat. His eyes have gone hooded, his lips curved slightly as he looks at me. As he *sees* me.

And, for the first time, I really see him.

Knowing that I'm skittish, Paul takes one careful step closer to me as he says, "My first priority has always been the pack. I'm an Alpha. It's part of the job description. But, when I saw you... for the first time I wanted something just for me."

"Paul..."

Another step. And another.

Before I know it, I'm walking to him.

I don't know if it's my omega nature that lured him in. Maybe it's his alpha side, his pure animal magnetism that makes him irresistible. Whatever it is, I'm lost in his gaze, allowing him to gather me up in his arms even as my wolf whimpers that this male... this male might just be the one to heal her broken half.

My wolf is enamored with Paul's. My human half yearns to throw her arms around his neck.

So I do.

Paul doesn't take. He doesn't demand. He meets my

eyes, searching, getting the answer from both my wolf and me. When we say yes, only then does he lower his head and kiss me.

As his soft lips slowly press against mine, I can't help but remember how Jack kissed me once and the bastard bit right through my lip. He was always trying to mark me in subtle ways, even more proud of himself when it made me *hurt*.

Wrapped up in the Alpha of the Lakeview Pack, I ache—just not in the same way.

I didn't know it could be like this. He's gentle, but there's an authoritative edge to his kiss as he takes control and I gladly give it up. I'm not strong. I'm not reckless. I'm only brave when I have someone else to protect. I'm made to be dominated, but as Paul encourages me to open up so that he can deepen our kiss, it hits me for the first time that there are different levels of dominance.

An alpha doesn't have to be cruel to control. He just has to be strong enough to catch you when you fall.

And, Luna help me, I think I've been falling since that first slice of cake.

Paul's the first one to break the kiss. I almost expect that, but I'm out of breath and secretly pleased when he dives back in for another. His arms link up behind my back, holding me to him in a way that leaves no doubt in my mind that as protective as he is toward me, that's not the only feelings he has.

We're both gasping when Paul moves so that his cheek is pressed against mine, his hot breath caressing my ear.

He doesn't let me go as he whispers, "I want you in my cabin. Not because you're an omega wolf. Not because of your pup. I want you in my cabin because, when I look at you, my instincts all roar *mine*."

I squeeze him tighter. My heart stutters as reality sets in. "But I'm not your fated mate."

I can't be. The Luna gave me to Jack, and if I never figure out what I've done to deserve that fate, I'll know that it must've been pretty awful.

Paul jerks his head back, searching my face again. I don't know what it is he sees now, but he leans in, pressing his forehead to mine. "So?"

Can it be that easy?

"I choose you, Janelle."

Paul seems to think so.

If only I could be so easily convinced.

I'm not all that strong so when I move my hands between us, using the flats to push against Paul's chest, I know he only steps away from me because he's allowing me to move away from him.

But I don't leave the side of the lake. This conversation isn't done yet and we both know it.

Stubbornly, I point out, "You can choose anyone."

"I could." Paul nods, the front strands of his shaggy, sandy brown hair falling forward. Unwilling to break eye contact with me, he shoves it out of his face. "And I'm not pushing you to say yes. A female like you, you deserve to be wooed. Courted properly. I'm just begging you to stay a little longer. Don't leave the den. Not yet."

Is that all? Paul seems to be saying it is, but I'm not sure.

"I don't know—"

And that's when Paul drops to his knees. The earth seems to shake at his sudden fall, or maybe that's just me.

A hint of humor brightens his dark eyes.

My face flames. "What are you doing?"

"Told you, Janelle. I'm begging."

Oh, my *Luna*.

"Get up," I tell him quickly. "Someone might see you."

"And?"

"Paul, you're the *Alpha*."

"Right. And my packmates know that there isn't a damn thing I won't sacrifice for the happiness of the pack. But, if just this one time, I'm not thinking about the pack. I'm thinking of my own happiness. You make me happy. Luna knows why, but from the moment you went for my hind leg instead of my throat, I've been drawn to you. You make me want to be a better male. For you. For your Gemma, too, but mostly for you, Janelle."

I don't tell him that the only reason that I didn't go for his throat is because I knew it would do no good. That night, I *was* feral. I *was* a true wolf. I would've killed him, only regretting it once Gem was safe.

Of course, now I'm glad I didn't. There's something so incredibly amazing about this male, and not just that he seems to want me. For Luna's sake, he really is begging. On his knees and everything.

He says he wants to be a better male. I don't know if that's even possible.

"Please, Paul." It comes out as a shaky whisper. "Don't do this."

"Then say you'll stay."

"Paul—"

He lifts up his hands. He's got them clasped together, a smile tugging on his lips. But his eyes? The humor has faded. Looking into them, I see his wolf staring back, seriously pleading with me to stay with him.

I join him on the ground. Hesitant but hopeful, I walk towards him on my knees.

He folds me in his arms, pulling me up against his chest again.

Leaning my cheek on his shoulder, I murmur, "You know this is a bad idea."

"I respectfully disagree."

"You could meet your fated mate tomorrow—"

His big hand lays gently on my back. When all I do

is tense, he pauses, but I let out a little of my inner wolf. For so long I was careful not to use my nature against other shifters. I didn't *want* Jack responding to it, and Paul deserved to know *who* I am before the realization of *what* I am changed his perception of me. I was so afraid that I'd lure him closer without meaning to, and as I show him my wolf, I know that I haven't.

I am now.

I'm okay, I tell him wordlessly. I'm okay.

He starts rubbing my back. "I could," he says softly, "but it wouldn't change a thing. I've already chosen who I want. And when she's ready to accept me, I'll mark her and I'll claim her and the moon will bless our mating. And then you'll be mine, and no one else will matter."

Right. Because it's not just Paul's fated mate I'm worried about. If only for a few moments, I managed to forget about mine—but it won't last.

I clutch him tighter.

"It's okay, Janelle," he murmurs. He might not use his wolf to soothe me, but his words have the same effect. "You don't think you're worth a second chance. I never thought anyone could see past my title. Maybe there's hope for both of us."

I hope so.

I really hope that Paul's right, too.

"If there is, I won't know unless I stay." I sigh. "So I guess I will."

For as long as Paul wants me to—for as long as it's safe for Gem—I'll stay.

I can't promise that I'll mate him. I can't promise that anything will pass between us other than the kiss outside of their treasured lake. I'm skittish and I'm broken and I'm terrified Jack will show up one day. Paul's determined to show me that none of that changes how he feels.

Still, there are so many things working against us.

But I'll stay.

And I do.

PAUL MIGHT HAVE BEEN ABLE TO USE HIS RANKING AT THE top of the pack hierarchy to keep his curious pack-mates from intruding on the den. He's the Alpha, after all, and what he says is law.

But he's also a younger brother, he tells me with a sheepish grin the next morning, and Corinne threatened to tell me embarrassing stories about when he was a pup if he didn't let her meet me sooner than later.

On the one hand, it's been a couple of days and I've already committed to staying here for the time being. On the other, I kind of really want to hear those stories.

In the end, I told him I was ready to meet Corinne, especially since she threw in an offer to show me how she makes strawberry shortcake if she got to come over.

The moment she walks into the den, a lot of things make a ton of sense. Right away, I'm met with a female who is a couple of years older than Paul, with kind amber-colored eyes, hair that's a shade darker than his—and an aura that's incredibly familiar.

She's an omega wolf like me.

No wonder Paul knows exactly how to react around an omega wolf with pups. His sister *is* one.

She's no pushover, though. After she gives me a once-over, gauging my mood, she pulls me into a reassuring hug, welcoming me to the pack before I can even think to put the kitchen table between us. She does the same for Gemma, tossing my squealing daughter in the air, never losing a step when Gem shifts mid-toss, another one of her baby dresses exploding over Corinne's head.

Paul's sister thinks it's adorable, and if she's surprised that Gem has such control over her shift, she doesn't say anything except to echo Paul's long-ago compliment: "What a cutie!"

He tries to get his sister to give us some space, but I'm pretty sure the word doesn't exist in the boisterous omega's vocabulary. Instead, she shoos him out of the kitchen, telling him that he can run along while she gets to know her new packmates.

Like her brother, Corinne has no problem claiming us.

Paul doesn't go, though. I'm pretty sure it's because he wants to be around to defend himself in case his sister really does start with the embarrassing stories, but if he's free to stay nearby, I'm not complaining. I... I really like having him around.

Gem does, too. He's so good with her. Compassionate. Generous. Playful. And, yes, goofy in a way that delights a pup while filling my whole chest with warmth—before making me hot in other places.

He encourages her to stay in her wolf form, teaching her tricks when it comes to stalking and tracking—things any wolf needs to know and that her father had neglected since she was "just an omega runt"—while Corinne bustles me into the kitchen to start baking.

The whole scene is cozy. For the first time in so, so long, I'm content.

No.

More than that.

I'm *happy*.

Of course, just when that thought flitters through my mind, something has to go and ruin it.

Not just something—*someone*.

A howl rips through the afternoon. It's a warning and a declaration all in one. The same howl I often

heard during the full moon right been an alpha challenge that left too many good wolves dead.

I know that howl. It haunts my dreams.

Jack.

He's *found* us.

9

Though it's been just about three weeks since I made my escape from the Wolf District, just like that I'm the same feral she-wolf who jumped into the raging river to avoid Jack's wolves getting their paws on my pup.

Saving my daughter is all that matters.

I'm out of the kitchen in a flash, running right toward the dining area where Paul is playing with Gemma. Both of them are frozen in place, heads turned in the same direction, ears cocked as they listen to the echo of Jack's howl.

At any other time, I'd think how my daughter mimicking an alpha is as adorable as it is worrisome; anyone looking would see that she's acting exactly like Paul. But not right now. I'm too concerned with getting to her before Jack can.

"Gem. Come here, baby girl."

My pup shakes off her stupor, bounding right over to me.

Paul glances my way. The terror in my eyes is plain to see.

"Corinne."

"Yes, Alpha?"

Alpha. Not Paul. Not baby bro.

She knows this is as serious as we do.

He gestures at Gem with his chin. "Take the pup. Keep her safe."

"Of course. Janelle? Tell Gemma to come to me."

Because Gem can tell that I'm losing it. She won't willingly leave my side unless I tell her to.

I've only just met Corinne, but I can sense that she's one of the few I would trust with my pup at a moment like this.

Nodding, I bend low enough to run my shaky fingers through Gem's fur before telling her, "Go on, baby. Mama says stay with Corinne, okay?"

She yips, obviously confused, but the fact that Corinne's another omega helps her decide. Even Gem can sense she's safe and after hurriedly rubbing her flank against my ankle, she trots over to Corinne.

Paul's sister picks her up, holding her close. "We'll wait right here, Alpha, until you tell us otherwise. Should I get the others?"

"Call Marcus. Tell him to be ready, but don't interfere unless Walker wins the challenge. Whatever happens, don't let him take them. Tell him to guard the girls, and guard the pack."

"I will."

It doesn't hit me that Paul's talking about what would happen if he lost an alpha challenge until he grabs my hand, squeezing it in reassurance. "Stay here, Janelle. Marcus is a good Beta. He'll keep you safe if I can't."

He can't mean what I *think* he means—

"Where are you going?"

Before I know it, Paul has dropped my hand, giving me one last lingering look before he backs toward the exit.

This isn't supposed to involve him. This is my problem. Jack's here to get to me.

But Paul is the Alpha of the Lakeview Pack. And as much as I wish it were otherwise, I know the meaning behind that howl.

It's a challenge, and he can't challenge me. Unless he's challenging my baby, there's only one alpha here who must answer that call.

No.

"Paul, no—"

"I have to. This is my territory. If Walker thinks he's going to challenge me, he's going to discover just how far I'm willing to go to protect it. Willing to protect *you*." His eyes lock on my face again, telling me more than he can with just his gaze. "I won't let him get you or your daughter. I promise you that, Janelle."

A promise is just words. He won't mean to break it, but with Jack out there? He might not have a choice.

I left my mate. I ran. Though the idea has my knees shaking, I know that if I don't face him now, I'm only buying time. He won't stop, and it's not fair of me to hide behind Paul when I know that I'm the one Jack's targeting.

Me and Gem.

"I'm going with you."

It's Paul's turn to say no. "What? No. I won't let him get to you. I promised you that you'd be safe here. I'm Alpha. I stand by my word."

He's more than that to me. I could care less if he was an alpha wolf, a beta, or even a delta. My experience with alphas has all been shitty—until him. His ranking in the pack hierarchy means nothing to me. It's just the *male* that I want.

Jack's taken too much from me over the years. I won't let him take Paul, too.

"Do you trust me?"

"You have my heart, Janelle. What kind of male would I be if you didn't have my trust?"

A foolish male, I think, since he's allowed himself to care for me despite my baggage and the risk I present to the rest of his pack. But even though it's been no time at all in the grand scheme of things, I also know that Paul is one of the best male I've ever known.

"Then, please. Trust me. I... I have to do this."

He runs his gaze over my face, trying to understand. Maybe he does. Maybe he doesn't. Though he tightens his jaw, like he wants nothing more than to order me to stay back, he nods.

"Okay," he says. "Just stay behind me, alright? When we meet up with Walker."

I nod. That's probably for the best.

"I won't let anything happen to the pup," vows Corinne.

Paul's sister has a swipe of flour on her cheek, but the friendly smile she'd been wearing all day is gone. In its place, I see a mother wolf who will do anything to protect a pup, even when it isn't one of her own.

"Thank you," I whisper before blowing Gem a quick kiss, then bolting toward the door.

Paul's already two steps ahead of me. He pulls it open, yanking it shut as soon as I run through it.

Before he can follow after me, I spin around, throwing my arms around Paul. I press the length of my body to his, nuzzling his chest with my cheek, rubbing my arms up and down his back. I throw every bit of my omega aura at him that I can spare.

He doesn't react. He just lets me molest him, sure that I must have my reason.

And I do.

I pull back, reminding him, "You trust me."

He tips my head back with his finger. "I trust you."

"Good. Now let's go."

I know instinctively which way to run. My shifter's hearing has already pinpointed where Jack's howl came from, but my wolf has always been able to sense Jack. From the moment he appeared in my home pack, claiming me as his fated mate, the thinnest of bonds had sprung up between us. It's so much weaker than it ever was—a new, stronger one taking its place, stretching between me and Paul—but it's still there.

By the end of today, it won't be. Either because I broke it or Jack did, I swear it'll be gone.

There are only two ways to get rid of it. So long as we haven't performed the Luna Ceremony, a bond can only be broken when one of the mates fully rejects the other—or one of them dies.

I don't know what's going to happen next, but that realization doesn't change anything. If I survive this, I won't be tied to Jack any longer. I've left him. Refused him. In all ways but the one that counts, I rejected him.

He's not my mate.

He's just a monster.

I wish he looked like one, though. I really do. As Paul follows my lead, knowing without acknowledging it how I'm able to race right to where Jack's waiting for someone to answer his challenge, I use the dwindling bond to bring us to the river border that separates the Wolf District from Lakeview.

Part of me expected that he'd be waiting near the hill that I spent all those days in. He's not. Instead, he's made his stand about twenty feet from the edge of the river at a different point entirely, yet firmly in Lakeview territory.

I should've known.

Paul told me that he went back to the cave where I'd stayed with Gem, marking it repeatedly until it smelled entirely of him; he'd done the same thing as soon as he figured out we were hiding up there, determined to conceal us from any predators who might be a threat to us before he could convince us to join him at the den. After I told him about Jack, he encouraged his enforcers to do the same. Over the layers of fresh urine, no one would ever be able to track us there.

He wouldn't need to use his nose to find us. Like me, all he had to do was acknowledge our bond. I guess he finally decided to come looking for us himself because there he is, looking as beautiful—and as dangerous—as ever.

The bastard has the nerve to smile enticingly when he sees me slow my approach, keeping a healthy amount of distance between us. And though his wolf would've caught the scent of Paul running with me, the smile develops a sharp edge when the dark-haired Alpha moves in front of me.

Jack's golden gaze flickers over Paul before it settles on me.

"I thought that would be enough to bring you running, my mate."

Not your mate.

I choke over the words. I want to say them, I want to *mean* them, but he's using his alpha nature against me. I can barely breathe, let alone defy him.

And, damn him, he's *enjoying* it.

Wearing that cocky, cocky smile I know too well, his gaze glances over me. Over Paul. He dismisses both of us quickly before his brow furrows. His smile wavers. "I don't see the little bitch. Where is she?"

Paul growls under his breath. Hearing him stand up for my baby gives me enough courage to peer up at Jack through the fringe of my eyelashes.

And I lie.

"She's... she's gone."

Paul goes silent. He doesn't even try to contradict me. He must really trust me after all.

Good.

"Gone?" Jack snaps. I've caught him by surprise. Thank the Luna. That might be the only advantage I have. "You mean dead?"

I swallow.

If it was anyone else, Jack would know that I was lying through my teeth. Alphas seem to have a sixth sense when it comes to people being untruthful, whether it's a scent thing or instinctual. I don't know. If I had the ability, I never would've left with Jack in the first place. As an omega, I can sense emotions and somewhat manipulate them, but when someone lies with such alacrity, I'm clueless.

But I'm also his mate—*unfortunately*. He's spent three years bending me, twisting me, breaking me to his will.

He'd never expect me to lie. It's how I was able to hide the truth about my pup as long as I did. Jack was too arrogant to think I'd ever dare lie to him.

I'm so freaking glad I thought ahead to rub my scent on Paul and his on me. I was banking on the fact that Jack wouldn't be able to recognize Gem's scent, and that he'd be more distracted by "his" female's scent mingled with another male's—and another alpha's.

He has no proof that Gem's alive. So, inwardly crossing my claws that this will work, I tell him that she's not.

"Yes." And, thinking of how terrified his threat made me, how heartbroken I'd be if anything happened to Gem, how I'll sacrifice everything to keep my daughter safe, I bring tears to my eyes. They're furious tears, but Jack's too much of a sociopath to tell the difference. "You bastard. You said you'd drown her, but you never got the chance, did you? The river did it for you."

It's obvious how little of a threat he thinks Paul is.

During a challenge, an Alpha will never take his eyes off of an opponent; it's a sign of submission. But as my angry words wash over him, Jack turns, appraising the rushing waters of the river behind him.

And then he shrugs. "You gave me one pup. You'll give me another. And, when you do, maybe I'll be gracious enough to forgive you for healing my marks."

Paul's rumble becomes a full-throated growl. "Like hell she will."

"Paul—"

Jack lets out a throaty laugh that has the hairs on the back of my neck standing straight. "I'll get to you in a minute, boy."

Boy, as if Jack is so much older than Paul. He's probably got five years on Paul, that's all, but it's not about age. It's about respect.

I tug on the back of Paul's shirt. Though he's bristling with rage on my behalf, he really is the perfect partner. Instead of snapping at me to get back, reminding me that I said I would, he nods.

I move to stand at his side. And then, using his strength to bolster my own, I dare to look Jack dead in the face.

"You're not my mate," I tell him.

His eyebrows rise. "Excuse me?"

The bond between us quivers.

It's never been strong; already the one that's been forming between me and Paul is twice as sturdy. I don't know why I've held onto it so long, but I know that I can't. Not any more.

So I let go of it.

"You're not my mate," I tell him again. Stronger this time. Undeniable. "You'll never be my bonded mate. I don't choose you, either, Jack. I... I reject you."

If only it was as easy as that.

"You're mine, Janelle." He laughs, like the idea of my actually having any say in my mating is funny. "Whose gonna stop me from taking what's mine?"

"Me."

"Paul, *no*."

I had hoped that Jack's challenge really had been meant for our daughter. When Jack barely paid any attention to Paul, I clung to that hope. And even if he did, that doesn't change who Paul is.

I'm an omega, but Paul Booker is an alpha. The Alpha of the Lakeview Pack. He gave me sanctuary and Jack is a threat.

I can't stop him.

As much as it pains me, I force myself to fall back as he moves in front of me again.

"This is my pack, Walker," he booms. "She's under my protection."

If Jack's surprised that Paul's accepting his challenge, he hides it well with his scoff. "Why are you wasting your time with an omega? She's not worth losing your pack."

"Who says I'm going to lose my pack?"

"When I rip out your throat, I'll fuck her over your corpse," taunts Jack. "She might think she can reject me, but she's mine. I'll bend her over, fill her with my seed, and wipe your scent off of her completely. Then I'll take over your pack and your territory."

I'm used to Jack talking like that. And I know that he means every word he says. Wearing Paul's scent to hide Gem's was a calculated move, but after all the time we've been spending together lately, it would've been embedded in my skin anyway. Not to mention that kiss...

I want to defend Paul. Tell Jack it's not what he thinks. That Paul and I have never mated. That he can't threaten the whole of the Lakeview Pack like that.

But then Paul steps forward and says solemnly, "A mate chooses. Any honorable Alpha knows that," and I keep quiet.

He doesn't need me to defend him. He's an Alpha. *My* Alpha. And he's going to defend me.

Another cocky smile tugs on Jack's lips. "I've never been honorable."

Paul bows his head, as if conceding the point. "Fair enough."

Jack's smile turns feral. "Never been fair, either."

"Good to know," Paul says conversationally a split second before he breaks into a sprint.

10

From one second to the next, Paul shifts from human to skin. Jack waits a beat before he shifts to his blond wolf, arrogantly proving to me that he still doesn't think he has anything to worry about.

That proves to be his undoing.

In his skin, Jack might've had the advantage. He's wider. Brawnier. And he's nasty to the bone. But as a wolf? As big as Jack's wolf is, Paul's is bigger. His grey wolf knows this land, too, and instinctually where the curve of the water is.

Jack doesn't.

It becomes clear early on in their brawl that he has some of his attention on the river at his back. It puts Jack on the defensive immediately. The seconds he wasted didn't help, either. Though the fight is furious, fur flying, blood spraying the dirt, it ends with Jack disabled on his back.

If the fight has anything to do with me, it's clear that Paul wants the victory more. But he's not vicious. If the roles were reversed, Jack would already have torn out his throat, but Paul hesitates.

No. Not *hesitates*.

Paul looks at me.

I know what he's asking.

The Wicked Wolf might not be honorable, but Paul is. And as much as I'd love to never have to worry about Jack again, he is Gem's father. My ex-mate. I'm an omega. I can protect those that I consider mine, but I'm no killer.

I shake my head.

Paul gives Jack's wolf a jerk, letting him know how easily he could end the challenge, then slowly eases his fangs out of Jack's neck.

Jack flips from his side to his paws as he snarls, but he's too late. The challenge is over. I know it. Paul knows it. Jack would deny it, but his wolf knows it, too. He could always issue another in the future, but for now, his wolf will go home to lick his wounds and his pride.

This won't be the last we see of him. I've never heard of Jack Walker losing a challenge before, and I can't imagine he'll be magnanimous in defeat.

He'll be back—just not for a while.

Paul stays in his skin as Jack leaps into the river, slinking away like a dog with its tail between its legs. He rests on his bloody haunches, a few stray blond furs clinging to his muzzle. I can sense his wounds, feel his pain, know that the challenge was closer than it appeared, but he refuses to move until his territory is secure again.

It's all I can do not to swoon.

Now *that*'s what I call an Alpha.

BY THE TIME I WALK BACK INTO THE DEN, PAUL'S WOLF at my side, Gem's in my bed, fast asleep.

I'm glad. The last thing I want is for my pup to scent both blood and her father on Paul. It would only upset her, and knowing she felt comfortable enough with Corinne to fall asleep while her father was on pack territory tells me all I need to know about the other omega.

She lets out a sigh of relief when it's her brother who is accompanying me back to the Alpha cabin. When she tells him that she'll call a pack meet and let the council know that, for now, the threat is over, she sounds non-plussed—but her eyes give her away. She would've gone as feral as I had if anything happened to Paul.

I'm still surprised when Paul nods, letting her go

handle things with his Beta and his council. In the Wolf District, only the Alpha had any control and I'm not used to the change. Things are definitely different in Lakeview—and, in my opinion, *better.*

I'm not used to it, but I look forward to getting used to it.

They take care of each other here. And, if I stay, they'll take care of me, too. Paul has. Corinne has. Countless packmates that I still haven't met have taken care of me all on the word of their Alpha.

Not because he ordered them to, either. But because he's a cherished Alpha, and they respect him.

Paul's done so much for me. Now it's time for me to do something for him.

As soon as Corinne leaves, I go into the bedroom to check on Gem. My pup is sprawled on her belly, snuffling softly as she dreams sweetly.

Good.

Paul's hovering in the doorway. Waving for him to come inside, I say, "Can you shift back to skin, please? I see blood on your fur and I want to make sure you're okay."

His wolf snorts, pawing at the hardwood floor as he shakes his head.

I roll my eyes. "Don't be a baby. You saved me from Jack. The least I can do is take care of you now."

Paul pauses, thinking it over. He cocks his head as if saying, "You asked for it."

He's right. I did ask for it.

My jaw drops.

I've spent my whole life as part of a pack. Nudity after a shift doesn't mean anything—and I tell myself that repeatedly as Paul goes from fur to skin and I get my first glimpse of a naked Paul.

It's not supposed to be sexual but, well, it is. With him, it totally is.

My eyes land on his cock. Even limp it's impressive and, as I stare, I watch as the thing starts to twitch.

Oh my Luna. What am I doing? Ogling the poor guy when I'm supposed to be checking his wounds.

I mumble out an unintelligible apology as I force myself to look away from his slowly growing erection; if I had doubts about any attraction between us, his reaction to my heavy gaze on his cock would be enough to wipe them away. This isn't about me wanting him or him wanting me. This is about me making sure my psycho ex-mate didn't hurt him.

His chest is covered in claw marks. His left cheek, too. I gesture for him to turn and he does. His back is bloody and bruised, though they're already fading. His ass... okay, I'm staring again, but it's freaking glorious.

Don't stare, Janelle. Don't stare—

My gaze shifts.

Okay. This? This I'm allowed to stare at.

There's a scar a few inches above the back of his knee. It's closer to his outer thigh, and it's a pretty solid circle. On closer look, I see that it's a ring of smaller marks.

Teeth.

Teeth marks.

It's a bite scar.

On Paul's entire body, there isn't a single marking. The reason for that is simple: no matter how brutal the injury, a shifter will heal. Unless they purposely choose to keep the mark, it'll be gone by morning.

A shifter can keep a mark in two different ways. One: a mating mark that is consciously kept as a sign that they've been claimed by their mate. Two: a shifter tattoo. A shifter tattoo is usually done by macho males who want to show off a particularly nasty wound they survived, usually from a challenge. By mixing silver shavings with a specific blend of herbs, the shifter can rub it into an open wound and leave a silverish mark on their skin.

Mating marks become white slashes in the skin.

And Paul's bite mark? It's white

I point. "Jack didn't do that."

Paul doesn't even follow my point. As if he's been waiting all along for me to see it, he simply shrugs and says, "Nope."

"And... that's not a shifter's tattoo, is it?"

Paul shakes his head.

I knew that, but I had to be sure.

He's an alpha wolf. Nothing should be able to mark

him. Except, perhaps, for a feral she-wolf protecting her pup—and only if he wanted it to stay.

I point at my chest.

He nods.

My legs buckle.

Paul is already moving toward me. Out of the corner of my eye, I see his semi-hard cock swinging as he lunges, prepared to catch me if I drop. I gasp—more because I've been trying to avoid staring at him like that while he's hurt—and he immediately backs off.

My whole face is immediately on fire. Mumbling something about getting a washcloth to clean his cuts, I dash toward the bathroom. By the time I've gathered together a soapy washcloth, a damp one, and a clean one so that I can wipe down the bloody gashes, Paul's found a pair of boxer briefs to cover up his cock. He's sitting in one of the chairs on the other side of the room, trying his hardest to seem non-threatening.

Yeah. It's not working.

Not that I'm scared. I'm both stunned and, okay, aroused. Because, whether it's on purpose or not, the tight underwear shows off his bulge—and the scar on the side of his thigh.

I don't know which one draws my attention more.

Both.

It's both.

I swallow, keeping my eyes on his face. It seems like the safest spot. "Uh. I know alphas heal even quicker than the rest of us shifters, but we should clean up some of the worst of those wounds."

He spreads his arms out. "My body is yours."

I make a strangled sound that has Paul quickly apologizing. "Didn't mean it like that, Janelle. Sorry. If you want me to clean myself up, I will."

"No, no. It's fine." Even though I know damn well he did mean it like that. He just didn't mean for me to squeak in response to it. "Let me know if it hurts."

He nods, and I get to work.

Most of the marks are already halfway healed so I tackle the worst. Before long, I realize that tending to the wounds is pointless and, instead, I focus on getting rid of the blood. And if I get more pleasure out of running the washcloths over his sculpted body than I should?

I can't help it, and I blame that mark on his leg.

My gaze keeps dropping to it. I thought I was being discreet, especially since Paul had closed his eyes while enjoying his sponge both, which is why I'm caught off guard when he rumbles softly, "It doesn't mean anything if you don't want it to."

I don't pretend to not know what he's talking about. And since I'm not ready to have this conversation, I give him one last swipe with the washcloth and pronounce him clean.

"I'll add these to the laundry pile," I tell him,

looking away as I snatch the discarded washcloths up. "I... thanks for everything—"

"You don't have to thank me."

Yes. I do. "Anyway, I'm exhausted. Since Gem's sleeping, I think I'm just going to turn in early."

"Sounds good. Me, too."

Phew. If Paul heads off to bed, that gives me at least another eight hours before I have to figure out what's going to happen next. It's worth sacrificing a meal to get my head on straight, I think as I toss the washcloths into the hamper, and I really need to—

I stop short when I see that Paul's already abandoned his chair. But he hasn't headed to his side of the Alpha cabin.

Oh, no.

Wearing only his underwear, he's grabbed a pillow from my bed, punching it to make it comfortable before he stretches out on the ground. He's not in my room, but directly on the other side of the doorway, on the edge of the dining area.

It's still the freaking floor.

"What are you doing?"

"What does it look like? I'm going to sleep."

"On the floor?"

"Mm-hmm."

"But why?" I'm flabbergasted. "Your bed's on the other side of the cabin."

"You're right. But this was good enough for me last

night. The night before, too. Every night since you've moved into the den, actually."

Ah, Luna.

He has to be kidding, only he's not... is he?

How did I not notice? I could use the fact that his scent covered every inch of his cabin, including the den, as my excuse. Or how just knowing he was near—but in the other half of the cabin—was enough to make me feel safe enough to relax in my borrowed bed. But I'm a shifter. I shouldn't have slept so soundly with a predator just outside my door.

Only... I haven't thought of Paul as a predator since the night I almost tore off his hind leg.

And honestly, I can't pretend I don't know what he's been doing. Even if Jack didn't do it right, I've watched enough female packmates be courted—been jealous of them and their devoted mates—to recognize the signs of a male performing his version of a shifter's mating dance.

I glance at his scar.

If asked, I would've said he began courting me that day at the lake. If pressed, I might've said it was the first time he brought food to the cave. But that mark? It just proves he's been at it for much longer than I thought.

And now? Now he's sleeping outside of my door, forever trying to protect me.

First he begged, now he's acting like my personal bodyguard after defeating my ex.

With a sigh, I gesture for him to stand.

He raises his eyebrows.

"Come on."

"Come on where, Janelle?"

He's really going to make me say it, isn't he?

"Look. I'm not going to let your pack think that I'm gonna stand by and let their Alpha sleep outside of my door. I didn't know before. Now I do. So, please, come inside. And before you ask, I'm not going to let you sleep on the floor in there, either. The bed's big enough for all three of us. Just... keep your claws to yourself, okay?"

My offer has surprised him, but Paul's not an idiot. He immediately gets back to his feet, stepping into the room as if worried I'll take it back.

As he shuffles past me, I hear him say off-handedly, "It could be your pack, you know. Just saying."

I close the door behind him. "And you would be my Alpha?"

"I'd be more than that if I could, Janelle," Paul says softly. At first, I think it's because he doesn't want to wake up Gem, but I know better. Especially when he says, "And I think you know that, too," I have to admit he's right. Deep down, I *do* know.

And... there it is.

After the evening at the lake, we've danced around

the topic, but he's never put his motives out there like that before.

Considering this is happening so close on the heels of Jack's appearance—and challenge—I have to ask, "Is it because of him?"

"The Wicked Wolf? Well, yeah—"

Because he wants to take Jack's mate as another "F-U"? I don't want to think so, but the niggle of suspicion won't leave me alone. The mark got my hopes up, sure, but his answer just sent them plummeting. "Oh."

"—but not what you think."

Hopes inch a liiiiiittle higher again as I chuckle weakly. "Am I that obvious?"

"No, Janelle. You're that beaten down. My wolf wants to see you protected, and I've been on board since the beginning." He gestures toward his thigh. "I mean, obviously. But that male hurt you—"

Stepping into Paul, I rub my thumb against one of the slashes in his cheek that hadn't quite healed yet. "He hurt you, too."

A crooked grin, so much more enticing than Jack's cocky smile. "He tried. But these marks will be gone by morning. The ones on you... they're buried too deep. I'd heal them if you'd let me, but I understand if you'd rather not."

"That other mark won't be gone by tomorrow," I whisper.

"No. It won't. And if it never becomes more than a

fond memory for me, that's okay. It was my choice to make."

Because mates get to *choose*.

He's not pushing me. He promised he never would. A mate gets to choose, and though that mark means he made his choice, it's all on me now.

I made the wrong choice once. When I let sunny Jack Walker sweep me off of my feet and carry me into his territory. But I also chose to leave.

Maybe, one day, I'll be strong enough to choose Paul.

"Let's sleep it off," I suggest. "We don't have to choose tonight, do we?"

He gives his head a slow shake. But he's still wearing his smile as he says, "I'm looking forward to sleeping in a bed again. With you? That makes it a thousand times better."

And if that's all I give him? He'll take it, too.

Because that's what a true mate would do.

11

Six months later

Paul is sleeping. Sprawled out on his belly, his face buried in one of our pillows, he appears dead to the world.

Appears being the key word there since, the moment I slide across the bed, his body stiffens; even asleep, he picked up on my bare skin rustling against the sheets. By the time I'm placing my feet on the floor, he's got his head turned my way, one dark gold eye peering over at me.

I gesture at the door. "I'm just going to check on Gem."

"You want me to?"

He's already starting to climb out of bed even before the question is out. That's Paul for you. It took a while for me to understand that he wasn't always offering to do things because he thought I was incapable—just another worthless omega wolf—but because he *wanted* to do things to help me. He wanted to make things easy for me because he was thoughtful and kind.

For almost six months now, I kept waiting for the other shoe to drop. Maybe living with Jack Walker had ruined me, but I was convinced that no one could be as perfect as Paul seemed to be.

Over time, I learned he wasn't actually perfect. He had a tendency to hover. He was incredibly overprotective, and after how easily Jack dismissed me, it was stifling. But as soon as he realized the effect it had on me, Paul apologized and promised he'd do better.

He did, too.

And it wasn't long that I began to accept that he wasn't perfect—but he was perfect for me.

True to his word, he's never pushed. From the first night that I invited him to sleep beside me, he's never left my bed. It was completely innocent at first, though. He never pushed, and when I finally decided I was ready to mate again about two months after I moved into his cabin, I had to seduce him. Considering I waited until the Luna was out, it was easier than I thought it would be, and Paul was everything I had dreamed of and more.

That was four full moons ago. Without looking for

my second chance, without trying to find a mate, it seems as if I stumbled on one anyway. He dotes on me, he adores Gem, and he's made it clear to Jack that I'm claimed. He didn't end my former mate during their last fight, but he's spread the word: if Jack comes back, he *will*.

Jack used to be possessive. Paul is protective. There's such a world of difference between the two Alphas, and my only regret is that it took me three long years to accept that the Luna got it wrong. I might have been fated to be with Jack, but I wasn't meant for him.

Then again, I think as I tiptoe into Gem's room, maybe she knew what she was doing. I suffered the entire time I was Jack's mate, but I left with my baby girl. Maybe Jack was the only male who could help me create my daughter and that was why the Luna partnered me with him in the beginning. If so, it was all worth it.

Looking at her, my heart swells. And I know that I wouldn't have changed a thing. The last three years were hell, but having Gem made it totally worth it, especially since it all led me to this moment in time.

I'm safe. My daughter is protected. I have a male who loves me and isn't shy telling me so. If I still haven't been able to say the words back? Paul understands. I eat with him. I sleep with him. I'm the one he defers to like no other, and the one he introduces as his intended.

And if I make him wait a hundred years before I accept him as my bonded? He'll do it gladly because it's what I want.

Only I don't want to make him wait. Not anymore.

The moonlight streams in through the window over Gem's crib. When we first moved her to her own space, my pup snapped at Paul's heels until he moved the crib closer to the window. She sleeps better when she could see the sky, I notice, and feel the Luna on her skin. It's definitely another one of her strange alpha quirks, but like all the others, Paul never said a word.

I finally confessed the truth about my baby a few days ago. I was almost sure that he already knew, but if I decided to accept Paul's proposal, I needed to be honest with him. Jack might believe that Gem drowned the night I left him—and I have no reason to believe that he thinks otherwise—but it's still getting harder and harder for me to conceal her true nature by myself. Eventually, someone else will figure it out, and I'll need help protecting her.

And if my instincts about Paul were wrong? If I needed to protect Gem from him? I needed to know that, too.

Whether Paul guessed or not, he took the reveal better than I hoped. He understood exactly why I kept it hidden, and he joked that the only thing that changed about our situation was that now he knew he'd have to watch out for the kitten when she got older in case she wanted to challenge him.

He was teasing, but later that night, he promised that he'd try his best to do the things for Gem that I couldn't. As an alpha, he could teach her what it was like to be that rank, something I never could've expected from Jack. Paul's been true to his word ever since, and though it's only been a few days, I already notice a difference. Gem is happier than I've ever seen her. Her wolf is calmer. It's easier to use my omega aura to hide hers, and it's all because she has another alpha taking care of her.

Now, with the Luna high in the midnight sky, it's time that I finally take care of Paul.

I tiptoe back into our room. I think about pulling on a sleep shirt or a robe before deciding against it. What's the use? I'd only be taking it off again shortly, and while shifters don't really pay attention to nudity unless it's sexual—and, yes, this is definitely sexual—I don't have to worry about anyone seeing us. The Alpha cabin is just as secluded as the one I had in the Wolf District. Only I was hidden away as Jack's mate there, but in Lakeview? It's a courtesy to their beloved Alpha, a sign of respect to give him and his chosen mate some privacy.

Tonight, we'll need it.

Paul's sleeping again. Snoring, too. For a moment, I smile to myself at the atrocious noise. Seriously. He sounds like a chainsaw going to town on a thick oak —and I can't help but find it adorable. That he's content and secure enough with me and Gem in the cabin that, if only for a few hours, he can let himself relax.

I almost leave him to his rest. Ever since Jack first broke through the border of Lakeview, Paul's kept the pack on high alert. He's such a good Alpha, too. He doesn't expect anything of his Beta or any other pack-mate that doesn't do himself. Half the time, he's patrolling the border in his fur on his own, almost daring Jack to come back.

He needs his sleep, but I'm pretty sure he won't mind waking up for this.

I move to his side of the bed, positioning myself so that the moonlight silhouettes me against his window.

"Paul, honey?" My voice is low. Soft. Even so, his snore cuts off right away. I wait a moment, then say, "You awake?"

Like before, he turns to look at me. His eyes are alert, but I watch as they glaze over with lust as he notices that I'm standing here naked. "Uh, yeah. I'm up. Janelle... wow. Uh... is everything okay?"

I smile at how flustered he is. This isn't the first time he's seen me naked—that honor goes to the time I shifted from fur to skin and made him almost forget about the dress he brought for me—but he makes me feel beautiful every time he does. Skipping over his words like that? It only makes me more confident in my decision.

"Everything's perfect," I tell him. I gesture behind me, fighting back the urge to giggle when his eyes follow the rise and fall of my boobs as I point out the window. "It's the full moon."

I don't have to tell Paul that. Like the rest of us, he knows. The Luna affects him, too, though in only the best of ways. He's a cuddly wolf who overcompensates for his desire to take care of his pack by cooking elaborate meals in the days leading up to the full moon. He runs countless patrols, trading off with his Beta, Marcus, and he spends hours mating me once he was sure of his welcome.

But he's never marked me. Even at the height of our mating, he's never broken skin even if it drives me wild to feel his canines grazing my shoulder, his claws caressing my skin.

That's going to change tonight.

I crook a finger, then turn away. Another smile when Paul can't quite stifle his moan at me showing him my ass.

"Come with me."

I'm not an alpha. I'm not bred to make demands. With Paul, though? When we're alone together, he likes it. He likes having the mantle of Alpha removed from his shoulders if only for a few hours, and it turns him on to watch me take the lead.

He's jumping from the bed so quickly, I hear a thump, then a muffled curse as he trips over his big paws in his haste to chase after me. That's probably my fault, too, since I gave my hips a little extra wiggle.

Like a lovesick puppy, my big alpha wolf trots after me as I slip through the rest of the cabin, bringing him to the front door. He murmurs my name again, a question in the two syllables. I know what he's asking, and I nod before pulling open the door.

When I was a young wolf, I dreamed of my mating night. I never expected that I'd belong to an alpha—let alone an *Alpha*—but the Luna Ceremony works the same for all of our kind. Just because the pack Alpha taking his mate, forming the Alpha couple, is more of a pack affair, the actual bonding is pretty simple.

I didn't need a big party. Some wolves treat their matings like a human wedding, but I never understood that. When I accepted a mate, I wanted it to be private.

Paul feels the same way. It's something we've talked about before, mainly because his way of leading the Lakeview Pack is so different than anything I'm used to. He might be the Alpha of the pack, but to him, that just means that he feels more responsibility to every packmate. He's not their ruler. Not their king. He proved that when he refused to take just any mate after his Alpha Ceremony. He even decided against learning the identity of his Luna-fated mate. He wanted the choice—and, to my everlasting surprise, he chose *me*.

Now it's my turn to choose him.

That's the first condition of the Luna Ceremony.

First, we choose.

Mating comes next.

Last? If there's not already a permanent mark, on the night of the full moon, we leave them on each other.

Paul already wears mine. Whether in his skin or his fur, he has the imprint of my bite mark on the back of his left leg. It was a shock to find it after his fight with Jack because I was only getting to know him while Paul was already ready to accept me as his.

For some reason, he was sure that we were meant to be mates from the beginning. Why? I'll never know, and I won't waste time trying to figure it out. As it is, I think I've wasted too many years. Now? I'm looking forward to forever.

And forever? It starts tonight.

The moon hangs over our heads. She washes us in her glow as I lead Paul behind the cabin. For the Luna to give her blessing, the ceremony just has to be performed when she's completely full. I'm not taking any chances. If the ritual calls for mating under the moon, that's exactly what I'm going to do.

It's the same with consent. Both mates have to choose, and though I know how Paul feels, I'm ready to share with him what my feelings really are.

I turn around slowly. He's right behind me and,

before he can step back and respectfully give me some space, I move into him until our bodies are pressed together.

He just about stops breathing.

Though Paul's encouraged me to tap into my feral side whenever I want to, I'm still an omega through and through. It's easier for me to follow his lead, and that's the same when it comes to mating. This is the first time I've been this bold; even my fumbled seduction a few months ago had me being the more submissive wolf. Tonight's different. I know it. He knows it, too.

He's already hard; this close, I can feel his erection pressing up against my naked belly. Honestly, he's probably been hard since our mating earlier before we settled down for bed. A gentle, attentive lover, he can go on and on, only stopping when I've been satiated. The full moon has him primed and ready to go, but unlike my former mate, he would never dream of searching out another female even if we're not bonded yet.

That changes now.

"It's the full moon," I whisper again, tilting my head back so that I'm looking directly into his gold eyes. I lift my hand, stroking my finger along the edge of his tight jaw. Poor guy. He looks ready to explode. Taking pity on him, I decide not to draw this out. "Are you sure you really want to bond with me?"

He exhales roughly. There's no malice in the sound, though. No. Just pure relief. Raising his eyebrows, he peers down at me with a whisper of a grin tugging on his lush lips. "You're kidding, right?"

"I'm just checking."

Lowering his head, Paul nips at my lip. It's teasing. Playful. I tilt my head further and he turns the nip into a deep kiss that has me clutching at his sides by the time he breaks it.

"Does that answer your question?" he rumbles softly.

"Maybe you should kiss me again so that I'm sure."

It was a tease, but Paul takes advantage of it anyway. As he slips his tongue into my mouth, stroking my tongue with his, he places his hands under my thighs. I swallow my gasp as he hoists me up, encouraging me to wrap my legs around his slender torso.

I brace myself on his shoulders as our kiss deepens even though I know it's not necessary. Paul has proved before that's strong enough to carry me easily and he'd rather cut off his right paw than drop me and see me hurt.

I can't get close enough to him—until I remember that I'm naked. He's naked. I'm sopping wet by now and Paul? If he told me that was an iron bar prodding my inner thigh instead of his cock, I'd believe it, he's so damn hard.

I press my hands against his muscular chest, giving

me enough space before our inevitable mating. Sex is one thing. Fucking another. But right now? I'm looking to bond with this male, and I need to make sure we're on the same page.

"I'm serious, Paul. It's the full moon. The Luna's watching. I... I'm making my choice. If you want to back out... if you want to tell me that you need more time... let me know. There's no going back after this."

The look he gives me is full of both heat and humor, as if he can't believe I'd even think to say that. And then he says, "I always knew I was waiting for the one who would complete me. You, Janelle... you complete me. And if you're willing to bond with me, I'm not gonna look a gift horse in the mouth. Unless you hit your head or something." His brow furrows, dark gold eyes still bright as he says, "You didn't, did you? Hit your head?"

Laughter bubbles up and out of my throat. "No."

"No concussion?"

"Uh-uh."

"And you still want to bond yourself to me forever?"

Darting out my tongue, I lick the same spot on his jaw that I'd been stroking a moment ago. "That's the plan. If you'll have me."

"Feral wolves couldn't drag you away from me, my love. You and our Gem. I'll do anything for my girls, whether you bond to me or not, but if you're saying yes..."

I throw my arms over Paul's shoulders, linking them by grabbing one wrist with the other hand.

"My daughter loves you," I tell him. Then, taking a deep breath, I admit, "I do, too. Yes, Paul. *Yes.*"

That's all I had to say.

He grabs his cock by the base, angling it until it's nudging at the entrance of my pussy. I move my hips, guiding his length inside of me before I sink all the way down on him.

Paul sucks in a breath as I squeeze him tight. Then, before I have to beg him to move, he grips me by my ass, lifting me up and letting me fall as he jerks his hips up at me.

Since we started mating, I've grown a little more adventurous. It's easy when you have a partner as caring as Paul. He didn't care that I'd had some experience, if only with Jack. I was secretly—and, yeah, *selfishly*—pleased to learn that I was his first. Neither of us had had a partner that we chose, and we learned the joys of mating together.

With Jack, my pleasure was an afterthought. Paul made it a priority. And if I have more than a few hangups from my time as Jack's mate, we've found ways to work around them. Though he'll take me from behind if I ask him to, it isn't often. He prefers to mate me face-to-face so that he can watch me come, and I love watching the look of concentration on his face as if it matters.

Just like now.

I blame the moon. We can usually mate for hours, exploring each other's bodies while Gem is sleeping and we have some time to ourselves. We did earlier this evening, but now?

I can already sense my orgasm closing in on me. And from the way Paul's breath has picked up as he thrusts into me, I know he's just as close.

"Mark me," I pant as I bob up and down on his powerful cock. "Make me yours."

"How?" It's a grunt, and the only word he can get out between his gritted teeth.

Even now, he's giving me control. He could mark me with his fangs or his claws, it doesn't matter so long as he marks me, but he's letting me choose.

But I don't need to. "However you want."

"I'll be discreet," he promises. "And I'll try my best to make it not hurt."

I'm used to hurt. I'm not worried about a few seconds of pain in exchange for a lifetime as his bonded mate. But discreet?

Screw discreet.

"Don't hide it. Mark me where it shows."

Sweat has turned his sandy hair dark. I can feel him swelling inside of me, ready to come, but he stops thrusting as soon as he understands what I'm asking of him.

Instead, he wraps his arm around my lower back,

holding me against him, as he gasps out my name. "*Janelle*."

I know what he's trying to do. Though I've spent the last six months careful not to compare him to Jack, I haven't always succeeded. This is Paul trying to prove to me *again* that he's nothing like my former mate. The asshole who wanted to slice open my cheek, then keep the marks. The bastard who thought of me as property.

When it comes to this male, though, I want to be his.

I grab him by the back of his neck, bringing his lips to the point where my neck meets my shoulders. My intentions are clear. I'm telling him that I want him to mark me, and I mean it when I say it needs to be visible.

"I want this. I want you. And I want every fucking shifter to know that I'm yours."

I know it's not the curse word *specifically* that does it. It's the certainty underlying my pleading. It's how much I want to belong to Paul, and how he can sense that I mean it. But when I murmur 'fucking' in his ear like that?

He pulls out just enough, slamming his cock back inside of me a second before he buries his canine fangs in the base of my throat. The pain mixed with absolute pleasure sends me over, my orgasm covering any discomfort as he digs his fangs in deep, grinding his pelvis against mine as he finally comes.

His moan is muffled by my skin. I shudder, letting out a low cry that is more of a prayer to our goddess than anything else.

It's done. The Luna Ceremony. Like the bite mark I've left on his thigh, I'll wear Paul's mark proudly for the rest of my life. Nothing but death can separate us now that we're bonded.

Jack can't. That's all that matters to me. Now that we're bonded, I don't ever have to worry about him coming after me again.

And we are bonded, Paul and me. I... I *feel* it. As he withdraws his fangs—while keeping his cock buried deep inside of me—I feel the unbreakable bond snap into place. It's like a piece of me that was battered and bruised and broken is finally whole again.

Complete, I think.

Paul nuzzles the mark he left in my skin, using his tongue to lap lovingly at the wound that will be a scar by morning, and I'm finally *complete*.

EPILOGUE

Twenty-five years later

After Paul finishes saying goodbye, he hangs up my phone and hands it to me.

"She called," he says gently.

I nod. "Thank the Luna."

It's the agreement we made with our daughter when she moved into that vampire city of hers. After her arranged mating with the Alpha of the Mountainside Pack fell through, I wanted Gemma to come back home to live with her father and me. She wasn't having it, though, and like so many arguments between my hotheaded girl and me, her father had to step in.

Poor Paul. He's been playing referee between the two of us since she first started to talk in complete sentences.

As my mate, he's predisposed to take my side, but as an alpha, he usually understands Gem's point of view in a way that an omega never can.

In last year's instance, he was on my side. He felt guilty that the Wolfson boy rejected our daughter, especially since he was the one to agree to their mating in the first place. Alpha to Alpha, he gave his blessing and let our daughter trade Lakeview for Accalia only for her to leave her intended a month after her arrival.

I'm glad it took her only a month to discover that he wasn't the mate she thought he was. For me, I wasted three years, and I've purposely kept an eye out for Jack Walker over the two and a half decades that have passed since.

Still, when Gem left Accalia, I didn't see why she couldn't come back home. Paul told her the same. But then she said the words I've been dreading to hear since she was a pup: "Mom, they know I'm an alpha."

She could always come home again, but I didn't push it after that. Every pack in the States is its own secluded community where the territory is guarded fiercely. I know that. I also know that no one gossips like shifters. If the Mountainside Pack knows, it's only a matter of time before it spreads.

And if it gets back to Jack—

I finger Paul's bite at the bottom of my neck. The marks are faded white scars that stand out against my skin, and even after all these years, I still get a sense of comfort just by knowing they're there.

Paul watches as my finger disappears beneath my hair, stroking his mark.

Shifters don't age the same as humans. Though we're not immortal, it isn't unusual to make it to two centuries. I'm only forty-eight now, Paul just shy of fifty, but he looks almost exactly the same as he did when I met him all those years ago.

He's just as strong, too. Scooping me up in his brawny arms, Paul holds me close before taking my seat on the couch. He settles me in his lap, wrapping his arms around me.

Just like always, my mate knows exactly what I need.

"Oh, Janelle, my love." He nuzzles the top of my head with his chin. "She's going to be just fine."

I want to believe that. It's why we made the arrangement in the first place. Gem could stay in Muncie, but I expect to hear from her around every full moon. As she grew older, her dominance was undeniable. Following my lead, she had to *act* like an omega so that no one would ever guess she was alpha. From her appearance to the name I gave her after we escaped the Wicked Wolf, she's been able to fool everyone into believing she's someone else.

But all it takes is one slip-up, as she proved when she let her temper get the better of her. Now all of

Accalia knows, and I'm terrified that she won't be able to dodge the same bullet I did.

My biggest fear is still Jack, but not in the way it seems. I never want my daughter trapped in a mating that she can't get out of. If any male shifter discovers that she's an alpha female, I have no doubt in my mind the lengths they'll go to bond such a powerful female to them.

I worry every full moon that this might be the time that she's forced to perform the Luna Ceremony. For twelve months now, I've been a bundle of nerves as I wait for her call to assure me that she's doing just fine on her own.

This one was different, though.

I lean my cheek against his chest. Just being close to Paul has a calming effect on me. Turns out, while the pack Omega can soothe the most feral beast, it's a devoted Alpha that does the same for me.

For the last year, I hoped that Gem had gotten over the bastard Alpha that broke her heart. I've known since she was fifteen that she was set on eventually mating the Wolfson boy, and when he became Alpha almost a year and a half ago, it seemed like she would finally get her wish.

Then he rejected her, and I've had to try to comfort my daughter from two hundred miles away. When Gem was still a small child, Paul—along with his pack council—made the decision to relocate the Lakeview

Pack to another lakeside territory closer to the East Coast. It was a way to put some distance between us and Jack, and that seemed pretty necessary if only because of his reputation.

Once we were bonded, my ex-mate seemed to back off. *Seemed* to. I don't care if it's been twenty-five years or two weeks, I can't trust that male. I've learned that from experience. The more space between us, the better.

But we're still far enough from the Fang City of Muncie and the Mountainside Pack that borders it. And now, after countless phone calls where we pointedly didn't mention her broken mating, my daughter is telling me that her fated mate—the same male who *rejected* her—is back, sniffing around her.

I sigh. "He's going to hurt her again. I know it."

"Gem's a strong female. I'm worried about *her* hurting *him*."

Normally, Paul's teases are enough to bring even the smallest of smiles to my face. Just... not now. I'm too worried for my baby girl. "She's too young to be dealing with this."

My mate's a smart male. He doesn't point out I was three years younger than Gem's twenty-six when I bonded myself to him. Instead, he says, "Maybe when he first asked to make her his intended. But she's a tough kid. I think she knows what she's doing."

I'm not so sure. Gem's convinced that she should

give Ryker Wolfson the time of day if only because she was named his fated mate. And I get it. I do. I mean, been there, done that, right?

Oh, my poor girl...

Pulling away from Paul, I look him right in the same familiar eyes I've lost myself in a thousand times over the years.

"The Luna doesn't always get it right," I remind him.

I don't mention Jack.

I don't have to.

Paul presses a sweet kiss to my lips. "You're right. That's why we get to choose. And, well, it's our little kitten's turn to choose."

He's right, too.

I chose Paul. It was the best decision I've ever made.

Now it's Gemma's turn to decide what she wants.

My little girl is all grown up. No matter what she chooses, we'll be there to support her.

Because we're family. We're Pack. And that's what we do.

AND... THAT'S IT ALL FOR JANELLE AND PAUL (EXCEPT for a few appearances in the main series)! The two of them have spent the last twenty-five years happily mated while also helping Gem hide her alpha side. Now it's up to the fully grown alpha female to find her own mate and discover if—when it comes to her and Ryker, her fated mate—the Luna got it right, or if she needs to choose her own mate.

Plus, if you think that Jack Walker actually gave up on his alpha daughter that easily... yeah. Revenge is a dish best served cold, and the Wicked Wolf of the West can be *very* patient when he wants to be.

Find out what happens to Gem next in *Never His Mate*, the first full-length book in the Claws and Fangs series! Keep clicking for a sneak peek at a grown-up Gem, as well as more information about her series.

After my mate rejected me, I wanted to kill him. Instead, I ran away—which nearly killed *me*...

A year ago, everything was different. I had just left my home, joining the infamous Mountainside Pack. The daughter of an omega wolf, I've always been prized — but just not as prized as I would be if my new packmates found out my secret.

But then my fated mate—Mountainside's Alpha—rejects me in front of his whole pack council and my secret gets out, I realize I only have one option. Going lone wolf is the only choice I've got, and I take it.

Now I live in Muncie, hiding in plain sight. If the wolves ever left the mountains surrounding the city, I'd be in big trouble. Luckily, the truce between the vampires and my people is shaky at best and Muncie? It's total vamp territory. Thanks to my new vamp roomie, I get a pass, and I try to forget all about the call of the wolf. It's tough, though. I... I just can't forget my embarrassment—and my anger—from that night.

And then *he* shows up and my chance at forgetting flies out the damn wind.

Ryker Wolfson. He was supposed to be my fated mate, but he chose his pack over our bond. At least, he did—but now that he knows what I've been hiding, he wants me back.

But doesn't he remember?

I told him I'll never be his mate, and there isn't a single thing he can do to change my mind.

To Ryker, that sounds like a challenge. And if there's one thing I know about wolf shifters, it's that they can never resist a challenge.

Just like I'm finding it more difficult than I should to resist *him*.

---

* ***Never His Mate*** is the first novel in the *Claw and Fang* series. It's a steamy rejected mates shifter romance, and though the hero eventually realizes his mistake, the fierce, independent heroine isn't the sweet wolf everyone thinks she's supposed to be...

** Sarah Spade is a pen name for Jessica Lynch. If you like the *Claws Clause* series and would like to see a different spin on shifters and vampires—written in first person, and featuring fated/rejected mates—check out the *Claws and Fangs* series coming soon!

Out now!

NEVER HIS MATE

A SNEAK PEEK AT THE FIRST BOOK OF GEM'S STORY

I know what they see when they look at me.

Minimal make-up to highlight my pretty honey-colored eyes and my high cheekbones. The flats that make me seem more petite than I really am. I have my hair styled in loose, flowy curls, though I draw the line at a hair bow these days. I'm even wearing a floral-printed sundress putting just the right amount of leg on display for May. And, sure, it gets pretty chilly on the mountain at night, but shifters usually run hot. Me? I run hotter than most even when I'm not this pissed off. Now? I'm burning up, and a dress like this is exactly what they expect from the type of wolf I've spent my whole life passing as.

Everything—from the blonde curls to the dress, right down to the non-threatening flats—is designed to fool their senses. Even my name was picked to be as gentle as possible. Gemma Swann... who can be afraid of a pretty blonde called Gemma Swann?

I've been doing this my whole life. When I was too young to understand, my mother hid what I was. Now it's up to me. No one can know that I'm not an omega like she is, and even though I'm beginning to have a harder time staying in control, I have to remember that.

Good thing I have a *lot* of practice.

Shifters are unique among supes. We have two souls inside of one form: our human half and our beast. To make their wolves ignore what they can sense about me, I have to make their human halves believe what they see.

I'm a doll. A toy. So very breakable.

By the time they realize I've been hiding in plain sight, it's too late. The claws are already out.

At this very second, I mean that literally.

Now that my steering wheel isn't in any danger of being destroyed, I let loose my claws. Gone are the short nails painted in a prim shade of dusty rose pink. In their place, three-inch-long lethal claws curve around my fingertips, waiting to be used.

But I don't. Not yet. Not until I hear about his betrayal right from Ryker Wolfson's lips.

Like I said. I'm not a moron.

"Gemma." The way that Ryker says my name has always done something to me. He has this raspy voice that washes over me, making me want to curl up and purr like a house cat. "I wasn't expecting you."

Of course he wasn't. After all, this is the first time that I've come to his cabin and every single wolf in the room knows it.

"I need to talk to you."

"We're in the middle of something—"

Ryker lifts his hand. Shane goes quiet.

"I'm almost finished here," Ryker says to me. "We can talk then, unless it can keep 'til morning." He tilts his head slightly. "Can it?"

You know what?

"No. Sorry. I don't think so."

He searches my face. I'm not giving anything away, and he eventually nods. "That's fine. Why don't you wait for me outside and I'll come get you when the meet's done."

Wait for him outside? Luna forbid I get to sit inside and witness what happens when the inner circle gets together. And going into another part of the cabin? Of course that's out of the question since I'm not his mate yet.

If Trish is right, I might *never* be...

AVAILABLE NOW

IF YOU LIKE THE SHIFTERS IN CLAWS AND FANGS, CHECK
OUT THESE POSSESSIVE HEROES...

In a world where paranormals live side by side with humans, everybody knows about Ordinance 7304: the Bond Laws. Or, as the Paras snidely whisper to each other, the Claws Clause— *a long and detailed set of laws that bonded couples must obey if they want their union to be recognized.*

Because it wasn't already damn near impossible to find a fated mate in the first place. Now the government just has to get involved...

I remember—

Three years ago, Maddox Wolfe lost his mate. Since there's nothing more dangerous than a bonded shifter on his own, Ordinance 7304 gives him three choices: voluntary incarceration until he's no longer deemed a threat; a lobotomy-like procedure performed by government-employed witches that would dissolve his bond; or, most final, a state-sanctioned execution so that he could be with his mate again. And, while death held a certain appeal in the hazy days following the tragedy, Maddox had his family and his pack to live for. So, refusing to give up his memories of his sweet Evangeline, he chose to spend the rest of his days in the Cage.

I forget—

There's a hole in Evangeline Lewis's memory. The doctors tell her that it's normal, that she'll recover fully in time. After all, it's only been three years since the accident that nearly killed her. They never thought she'd wake up; a nagging, annoying sensation that something's wrong is the least of her worries. Especially since she has so much going on: a new apartment, a new job, her mother's well-meaning attempts at match-making... but tell *that* to her wayward psyche.

By day, she can't shake the feeling that something's

missing. And, by night, she can't escape the dreams of a shadow man with glowing golden eyes...

It's entirely by chance when Maddox's brother follows that familiar scent to the beautiful brunette with the haunted smile. But he knows immediately what he's found: Maddox's mate, alive if not altogether well.

Once he learns the truth, Maddox will stop at nothing to get her back, even if it he has to follow every twisted, convoluted letter of the ridiculous *Claws Clause* to do it.

Read all about how Maddox and Evangeline find their way back together in Hungry Like a Wolf!

.

KEEP IN TOUCH

Stay tuned for what's coming up next! Sign up for my mailing list for news, promotions, upcoming releases, and more!

Sarah Spade's Stories

And make sure to check out my Facebook page for all release news:

http://facebook.com/sarahspadebooks

Sarah Spade is a pen name that I used specifically to write these holiday-based novellas (as well as a few books that will be coming out in the future). If you're interested in reading other books that I've written (romantic suspense, Greek mythology-based romance, shifters/vampires/witches romance, and fae romance), check out my primary author account here:

http://amazon.com/author/jessicalynch

ALSO BY SARAH SPADE

Holiday Hunk

Halloween Boo

This Christmas

Auld Lang Mine

I'm With Cupid

Getting Lucky

When Sparks Fly

Holiday Hunk: the Complete Series

Claws and Fangs

Leave Janelle

Never His Mate

Always Her Mate

Together Forever

Hint of Her Blood

Claws Clause

(written as Jessica Lynch)

Mates *free*

Hungry Like a Wolf

Printed in Great Britain
by Amazon